CARDBOARD CITIZENS

by

Craig A Watson

Copyright © 2025 Craig A Watson

All rights reserved

PREFACE

Journey with Ana and Danny as they struggle for survival through a brutal world of psychosis and addiction. Where danger lurks round every corner. You could be maimed for a bottle of drink.

The chains of their traumatic pasts weigh down heavy, drag noisily behind them over savage city streets.

Flashbacks of war and abuse. Night terrors, delirium tremens constant bedfellows on the cold hard pavements at night.

But even in the darkest of places there is light at the end of the tunnel.

Never judge a person until you have walked a mile in their boots.

Will they have the courage to face their demons and triumph over adversity in a place where few escape?

CARDBOARD CITIZENS

PART ONE

Just like the sea that had left its residue of junk and driftwood high and dry after the storm, there were people too. Stark and ugly was the human wreckage. Also battered by many winds and tides, left broken and twisted by the storm of life. Left to wander alone along the blackness of the embankment.

Harry watched the green sea churn and swell, the current hammer ceaselessly under the pier as he stared across the channel. He had to catch his breath, he could see the rush and hear the roar of the waters. Its dark seething menacing mass rolling between its creaking timbers as the raging torrent gathered itself against the walls and hurled and spewed its raging muddy foam from underneath.

Three in the morning and silence descended upon the seafront. Only the breath of the dog on Harry's lap penetrated the great stillness marking the passage of time. Coils of fog grew along the hundred yards of sleep that stretched down the prom, licking the edges of their tents with tentacles of cold discomfort. The soft crackling of the oil drum fire settled and the flames faltered.

The yellow hues of the lamp lights just penetrated the mist like floating golden orbs. The dog now in deep slumber, its gentle breaths were soothing slowly lulling Harry to sleep. Not really sleeping but lazy and crippled from his anaesthesia, curled into a tight ball coiling the ugliness of his wounds.

As the solemnity of twilight drew in the silence grew deeper. The sounds of cars, the echoes of voices and footsteps muffled by the fog which hung over the camp like a misty veil slowly dissipated and Harry soon succumbed to sleep.

The twilight always began with the shakes, sickness and fear, Danny could feel the bile rising from the pit of his stomach. He dragged himself out of his tent, crawled into the gutter, gagged and shook before letting go at both ends. Black out.

Sometime later he regained consciousness and managed to stagger outside and onto the street before collapsing. Black out.

Coming back to his senses he was surrounded by an ice white brain penetrating light, which pricked at his eyes like hot needles. Slowly twisted black shapes loomed out of the white light.

Hideous looking creatures with mangled features and mangled limbs, grubby twisted caricatures all bent out of shape by life's pliers stared down at him through the fog.

Danny felt ashamed his clothes were rags stained with excrement urine and vomit clinging to his bloodied and bruised body. His head covered with bumps, cuts and scratches was fizzing his vision blurred and distorted like looking through a fairground mirror.

Yesterday's snow now formed streams of dirty brown slush on the pavement, which seeped through his split soled boots held together with gorilla tape.

The bitter south-westerly whipped around their flimsy plastic tents crying and moaning like a tormented spirit, howling through their ramshackle encampment near the sea.

Danny saw people sitting on abandoned broken furniture, some standing around and some lying on the ground, around a makeshift oil drum fire like a post-apocalyptic community.

Men and women with wet brains, collapsing veins, abscesses about to burst. Minds warped by addiction and psychosis trapped in their psychotic Punch and Judy sideshow. When the wind blew it lifted the ash from the fire and it spiralled and fell around them like grey burning snowflakes.

The alcohol poisoning cramps took hold again, draining the very life blood from within him. Turning Danny rigid with pain, building and coursing through his body with such intensity he feared his throat would split, his head unzip and his eye sockets rupture. His whole body spasmed sending shock waves to his brain, rendering him useless and immobile on the wet earth.

Gritting his teeth until the pain began to wane, ebbing and flowing like the tides of the sea .The noise from the traffic on the ring road which whizzed relentlessly seemed deafening, driving into his brain like the pneumatic drilling on the road works. The traffic exhaust fumes that hung in the air were choking.

Danny reached into his sock to take out his inhaler, shook it and tried to take a puff. To his dismay it had run out of spray and resorted to heaving up great heaps of phlegm instead. Black out.

~ ~ ~

Harry's dog stood stock still growling into the fog. The Intruder was something sinister, insidious. He braced himself poised for attack, straining his eyes through the foggy atmosphere gathering in clouds trying in vain to see the dog his eyes discerned nothing. The dog was hidden in the mist rooted to the spot. The force advancing the movement in the shadows was difficult to follow.

The veil of mist that hung over the camp like an ominous shroud was denser than mere fog. Clouds of darkness boiled within the field of vision weaving a pattern of dark purpose. Veils of black smoke swaying with long slow sinuous motion, rippling movement stalking its prey. Wave upon wave of exhaust fumes overwhelming and moving through the grim clogged air. Dark malignancy coming in waves as heat rolls of a furnace menacing and oppressive. Harry sat strung out like a piano wire tuned and screwed up to an impossible pitch, his nerves wrung out vibrating and excruciated.

Danny's brain snapped back to reality again from wherever he had left it and found himself still lying on the path , but now he was surrounded by the usual suspects. The local hoi polloi of junkies and alcoholic reprobates.

Cheeks ruddy and eyes dilating they shouted across the street and glared at each other psychotically. Slurping from special brew cans as exhaust fumes and fog dripped around them.

They were the roughest looking mob Danny had ever seen. They were all smashed out of their tiny minds even at this early hour. Truthfully Danny didn't know if it was six o'clock in the morning or six o'clock in the evening, he had lost all track of time and was living in a permanent, perpetual, procession of black outs. Black out.

~ ~ ~

Demonic shadows swung in on the breeze denser and darker, sentinel shadows of thick black smoke. Harry's heart murmured as the spectral chill transcended, tumultuous foreboding spread within him. The whole evil atmosphere surrounded him, casting him in its net like a hunted animal brought to bay. The unseen power full of malignant justice stretched out its cold tentacles. A tangible horror that couldn't be subdued, shadowy retribution from the other side watching and waiting.

Danny's mind Kept snapping back again with each returning ray of consciousness from wherever he had left it. Now lying on the path his face glued to the concrete with vomit. The stench of stomach acid within filled his nostrils and drooled into his brain, as he painfully tore his stubbly cheeks from its adhesive grip. His hair spread and stuck to his face with sick.

A girl stood next to him frozen like a statue in the park, her limbs fused and contorted at an impossible angle. She lurched and twisted her arms around the back of her head like an out of control robot, before collapsing to the ground in a twitching heap.

A man sat on a blanket drinking from a can. He looked at the woman shaking on the path. You could only wonder how much he was aware of anything, as he rolled blood shot eyes that had witnessed so much pain, loss and affliction.

There was a new arrival sitting on an upturned crate outside a white battered tent .He had a towel over his head and was sniffing from an aerosol can. He inhaled the spray and took the numbing effect. Another sat dribbling a lengthy drool from his mouth, eye balls sucked up to the top of his head. An old man curled up like a mongrel on the concrete, with matted hair and ripped clothing riddled with fleas, blood splatter over his face and most of his teeth kicked out from past adventure slowly dying an ugly death.

They were all on a long dark road nameless and without end. Seeing their lives through a thick mist of chaos marooned on the edge of society. Suffering from a hopeless condition of mind, body and spirit which they pursued to the gates of insanity and death.

~ ~ ~

The pusher gave Cameron the creeps and made his skin crawl. A resemblance to Charles Manson as he leered with his mad staring eyes. A sub-humanesque troglodyte, sunken cheeks teeth like a twisted car wreck. Bad breath and body odour poured profusely through his pock-marked pores. As he twitched and jerked about he demanded the money.

He said it was pure stuff best in the city, no talc or sugar in the mix. He took the money with his slimy paws. Stepping over some freshly made pavement pizza, passing a man heating scag powder through tin foil and inhaling the fumes through a plastic straw Cameron went back to his tent.

Cameron sat crossed legged on his mould infested mattress and loaded the hypodermic, just enough moonlight penetrated to see. The veins in his emaciated legs were hard to find. Kicking off his shoes and socks he gritted his teeth as he inserted the needle into the hard black skin on the soles of his feet trying to control his trembling hands then he collapsed on to the filthy bedding.

Soon he would sink beneath the surface where he would succumb to restful oblivion, the dissipation of pain, mental, physical and spiritual emptiness.

~ ~ ~

The rising moon cast its long ghostly shadow across the gaunt pale faces of the men and women, shuddering and dribbling in their various states of consciousness.

How many here who lay groaning in their sick beds were marked for death? While others who lay here yesterday are now laid up for burial.

There is a terror that strikes by night yet no one can see it. A pestilence that prowls in the darkness but no one can escape it. What are they but men and women condemned?

No shield can protect them from the dark angels blow, nothing can slake the fury of the grim reaper. Whom it lists it wounds and whom it wounds it kills. It takes many forms and like the devil himself respects no person.

Danny awoke. Ana was leaning over him. The twisted features on her alabaster face contorted into the image of Munch's scream as she started kicking him in the ribs.

"Need smoke."

"I've got none."

"Bull shit, please just one smoke."

"I've got none."

"Why not?" Her face flashed rage spitting out the words full of wrath full of venom. "*Kurwa spier dolic.*" Blasting him with a sewer breath and foul tongue.

"You're sick Ana you need help you're gonna die."

"Maybe better for me dead." Screaming, sweating, shaking, wild blood shot eyes full of fear, desperation.

"Think about your family."

"My family dead."

"They're not they're…"

"You know nothing of my person I better off dead."

Things never looked bleaker for Ana pregnant and addicted. The world had forgotten about her and left her to rot like the rubbish at her feet. Dirt and cuts were itching against her emaciated limbs as she stood shouting, shivering and slowly self-destructing. Drenched in the slag of the weather forecast dying in front of Danny's eyes.

"Please you get me spice."

"No."

"You no listen you no understand."

"Smoke that you'll kill the baby."

"I know my body not your body, bull shit."

An icy blast hit them like a freight train as she slumped towards Yuri sitting by the fire. Eyes wild and glowing in the flickering flames.

"Please you give me something I need."

"No money."

"Go come cash, come cash."

"Where?"

"Come cash come cash, hole in wall."

"No money."

"*Kurwa* Yuri just five pounds, I hungry I tired, maybe I die it cold fuck sake freezing look my face like baboon."

The argument was escalating beyond control, exchanging insults nose to nose spittle flying.

Harry lay cowering inside his tent. Every fibre of his being silently screaming mercy begging salvation. He sobbed barely able to speak gasping for breath, shaking to pieces. Perspiration seeping from every pore, frozen to the core. Jolts charged through his poisoned body, fear gripped him as the voices in his head grew louder.

Ana went to Cameron's tent and saw him lying on the filthy mattress, barefoot drooling shrouded in mist, unaware of the destruction of his body slowly prising apart in his sleep.

Ana stomped towards him angrily, she shoved him but there was no response.

"*Kurwa*." She raised her arms with frustration.

Delirium descended upon Harry slowly covering him like a sheet, his whole soul consumed by the demonic force. Dark shadows loomed, the feeling poured over him and through him like a great wave swallowing him deeper into the black abyss. Black enteritis pushed through the walls of his tent to claim his soul. Blinding flashes, wailing voices of the damned. Satan's mocking, trapped inside the darkest crevices of his fevered mind unable to be released, echoed around him dragging his wretched soul deeper down.

Evil descending, thrashing and weeping. Shadows are creeping, the devil is reaping.

Ana unzipped Harry's tent and stuck her head inside. Harry saw her approaching her eyes burning and two small horns protruded from her head. Caught in the imaginary vortex Harry's tent flapped in the cloak of death. A great rushing sound swept around him, something ethereal arose from the fog and shook his soul as the tempest shook the seas.

Staring into the void a countenance that was terrible in its ruin holding its discarnate force sucked him into the stream of the vortex. By slow degrees lurid elemental things manifest wrapped in sulphurous flames, phantasmagorical ectoplasm and demonic omnipresence he could hear its slithering hooves he saw Lucifer.

She returned back to Yuri. "Fuck you, fuck everybody."

Ana threw a hard punch and Yuri staggered back and collapsed on his tent. He got up grabbed her hair pulled her to the earth, Ana was biting and scratching like a wild beast.

An old man stood to the edge of the brawl and started jabbing at the air with his fists. He made punching sounds as he shimmied and ducked and weaved, waving his fists about in front of him. Throwing left and right hooks and uppercuts enjoying the fight.

Rolling on the ground like two horny foxes, Ana grabbed two jagged rocks off the ground. Ana swung her fists at Yuri's face, hitting him square in the chin he fell over. Ana rushed him, pinned him down and pounded his head with the stones like hammers, systematic and relentless in her fiery furiousity screaming obscenities. A cat fight to death in the snow.

Danny rushed in and tried to break up the fight managing to pull them apart and separate them. Yuri's grey hair turned copper as he slumped to the ground holding his bleeding head. Yuri crawled away through the ice, his eyes and nose streaming, his mouth full of salty blood he spat out a gob full of broken teeth.

The old man stopped punching the air and looked around in wind-blurred confusion. He went back inside his tent, started crying and wailing relentlessly into the night with the rage and despair of a tortured soul. Rising along with the shouting and screaming and oblivious noise-making.

Yuri crawled back inside his tent wrapped his head in a torn shirt to stem the flow of blood. He covered himself in blankets trying to melt the chilliness of the air. His body dripped with confusion and cuts. Under the covers he soon calmed, his sobbings grew weaker.

An immeasurable silence arose within Cameron as the heroin took hold an unfathomable sense of peace descended and transcended. Gradually soft luminosity filtered through an open door drawing him closer to the light. A ghost appeared enveloped in an opaque haze like a spirit wrapped in a watery shroud a palpable presence drew him closer. His head grew dizzy, choirs of angels fell upon his ears, seraphic notes poured forth, notes of haunting beauty. Euphoria. The calm swept over him and through him enveloping him pulling him closer. He surrendered to the celestial light

He departed this vale of tears.

~ ~ ~

The community support officer didn't look up from where she stood in front of the bench. She knew her regulars, she could tell who was who after all this time. Just by the sound of their shuffle, coat ruffle never mind a cough or sneeze.

She looked up from her note book and raised her eyes aloft as she regarded the three wise monkeys; cold starving and miserable slumped wretchedly on the bench. Hung over with the shakes, blood on their hands and faces brutalized by the drugs and drink.

Weary, desolate and forsaken. The waifs and strays of humanity in and out of the station's relentlessly revolving door. It was a grim night to be out. The rain was cold pitiless and increasing a dank keen wind blew across the street leading from the sea. The pavement was greasy, street lamps burned dimly.

An hour ago Cameron was zipped up in a body bag and taken away in the back of an ambulance. The small group of tents had been taped off and it whipped and fluttered in the breeze. Wet sticks hissed on the fire. The sweet and sickly aroma of marijuana hung in the air. The stink was tangible mixing with human and animal faeces, wood smoke and raw sewage that ran down the drain pipes flowed from a blocked drain and trickled in a stream across the alley.

A pile of rags sat on the end of the bench. The rags stirred and a white pock-marked face appeared. The creature coughed and she recognised his smell and rank wheezing breath. Waterhouse held out her hand like an old fashioned school mistress. He took the joint out of his mouth and threw it in the mud, his eyes followed hers with contrite hatred.

"Harry, your name's not on my list. Where were you at the time in question?"

"If it's a list which says we can shit on you from a great height and fuck you about for the rest of your life and screw you up and fit you up like a kipper, I fucking should be."

Harry's mangy dog, its rib cage protruding and chained to the lamp post struggled up on its hind legs and began to howl. She made a mental note for an animal welfare check, then turned her attention towards the scrawny little man sitting in the middle. A skeleton of a man, his hands and head wrapped up in a torn shirt. His left ankle red raw oozed blood and puss infected by the numerous times he injected into it. Next to him lay his battered rucksack tied up with string its contents spilling out onto the white canvas builders sack he used as a blanket, an assortment of spoons, citric acid and syringes some broken, some exposed bent rusty and caked with dried blood. She would throw it away before she left.

"Yuri, are you still with Ana?"

"What of this dumb whore?"

"She says you beat her."

"Crazy bitch. I hit her once I make mistake I was drunk I'm sorry. She hits me all the time."

Yuri pointed to different parts of his body. Scars and bumps a testament to Ana's violence laid bare. A scar on his forehead.

"She did this with rock." He pointed to his broken teeth like a car wreck.

"She knock these out with her foot" He lifted up his shirt and turned around and showed the scar on his lower back.

"She slash me with knife."

Lights flashed from car headlamps as they passed on the ring road. The beam swept past the railings and fell across them in a pale flicker, bleaching the camp like a negative. All pattern and colouration was obliterated and the people rubbernecking on the ring road were completely oblivious to their one and only chance of seeing them standing by the bench on their meaningless car journey.

A gust of wind picked up a million shopping bags, fast food wrappers and carton. They washed across the group of tents in a great tidal plastic surge.

"Ok guys you can fuck off now, I need to talk with Danny in private."

Danny just looked at Waterhouse; he didn't say a word he didn't have to. She knew his bones and the calcium and blood that swam within him.

"I want my life back," he said.

"You have a choice, you always have a choice."

"There not bad people they're just..."

"They're sick."

"They need help."

"You're important too. You have to walk away and look after yourself. No one can fix them, they have to fix themselves. They are responsible for their own lives and you're responsible for yours."

"Maybe."

"I lived with a drug addict for years, walk away while you still can, before they drag you down with them."

Danny kept silent.

"Danny I've got a letter for you."

"Is it an arrest warrant?"

"No. It's something you need to look at."

Waterhouse reached into her jacket pocket, took out a letter and passed it to Danny. Headlights flicked across the street and made their short journey from one side to the other, all pattern and colouration obliterated.

~ ~ ~

The yellow beam of Danny's torch stuttered and swelled in the darkness, throwing dancing shadows at the walls of his tent, as his hands shook. His nostrils detected the pungent smell of mould infested sheets and blankets.

He held the crumpled letter in his shaking hand but he dropped the torch and was plunged back into darkness. Danny lurched to unzip the tent just in time to retch in the gutter. Coughing and spitting he rested his head against the gritty surface of the pavement and looked up at the sky.

A thick blanket of black cloud slowly crept up covering the deep purple sky and the rain began to gently fall. A flash of dirty yellow lit up the clouds and thunder rumbled like God breaking wind in coalescence with an ominous rolling in his stomach like a writhing serpent.

Rumbles carried over the seafront the sound slowly drifting in and out gently stirring the winter breeze and the creatures within. Danny came back inside the tent and slumped back on the covers.

Moments later Ana burst in through the entrance and tipped a bag of fruit all over him.

"For you, eat."

"No you have."

"No not me you I no hungry go eat."

Danny began to eat.

"America drop bombs on Afghanistan ten thousand children dead, why?"

"Don't know."

"Adolf Hitler no my grandfather, me no Bosnian princess, you like food?"

"Yes thank you."

Another rumble of thunder. Danny felt his arthritic bones flare underneath his clothes. Felt ribs ache and the wind bellow over his back as he sat in the draft. Pistons raced exhaust pipes coughed on the ring road.

"Yuri punch me."

"I know."

"Yuri too much heroin."

Ana cuddled up to Danny and took his hand.

"Why you no wife, you beautiful face, maybe me your wife maybe marry."

"What about Yuri?"

"He doesn't matter my person."

"Harry."

"Harry dumb kopf too much speak too much yada too much Kojak too many questions. You stay with me. I look after you. Maybe you father for my son." She patted her stomach.

"Maybe." said Danny.

The smell of ammonia hung in the air, sirens blared and horns sounded all around them.

"You know I love your person," she said, stroking his arm and chest. "You give me everything, I pay back I promise one day you come to my home I cook for you"

"When?"

"You stay with me next merry Christmas in beautiful home. I help you I promise."

"Maybe."

"Danny please very much money for marijuana I stop two weeks I promise?"

"No you have to stop smoking this."

"Please very much."

"I don't like it when you smoke it."

"You no my husband you no tell me what to do."

"I don't."

"Ana no smoke no take heroin it's bad for you all the time."

"It is."

"Heroin bad yes. Marijuana good no stress."

"Makes it worse."

"No you no my psychiatrist too much speak zipper."

Danny caved in and gave her a tenner.

"No more. Food or smoke your decision."

Ana took the money, kissed him on the head then went outside.

The clouds burst and the rain began to hammer down on the canvas. Within a few minutes the blocked drain in the alley overflowed and flooded the street. The howling wind shook the blackened trees which loomed over the tents like the skeletons of sea monsters, twisted and mangled branches snapped and cracked in the canopy above their heads.

As the howling wind and thunder claps annihilated every other sound, as the water lashed down and the lightning struck electric blue and white, Danny took the crumpled letter from his pocket.

Nausea crept against his lungs as he sat in the blue flickering light speechless. Minutes passed as Danny sat staring blankly into space choking back the tears.

~ ~ ~

Ana stood motionless like a statue in the park, from somewhere she heard her Grandfather's voice calling beckoning her.

"Come out of the Forest, come out of the Forest, it's safe now."

The voices carried on the wind. The voices of her old friends and neighbours. Mothers and fathers, grand-parents calling their loved ones.

"Come out of the Forest, come out of the Forest, it's safe now."

Ana looked up into the gathering maelstrom, heard a loud rumble of thunder and saw a crack of blue lightning light up the night.

"Come out of the Forest," hauntingly echoed around her.

Suddenly she found herself in a light-filled forest. Her old childhood friends appeared to her down below by a stream lit up by the flickering blue electric light.

Ana felt an icy chill run through her veins; she couldn't speak her tongue was useless. She looked to find her old friends but was blinded by the hazy mist that hung around and clouded her view. Another crack of thunder. The power surged through her toes and limbs and put a tight grip round her throat.

The other side of the ridge cut off from her friends she counted the seconds between the thunder and lightning watching them.

"*Novak.*" Someone shouted. "*Novak.*"

"*Papa. Papa.*"

She looked to see her little brother splashing through the water, running to her grandfather saw a bullet rip his throat wide open and spill his brains against a tree. Ana's face distorted, her mouth twisted into a gaping black hole and she screamed an agonizing scream.

The storm produced a billowing roar which shook the earth beneath her feet. Slowly the vibrations mellowed in intensity and the rain began to cease.

Gradually she heard the overhead noise of a helicopter which built to a deafening crescendo as it hovered over the ring road. The air vibrated between its rota blades like the amplification of wasps. A colossal beating wave that continued for minutes, projecting a beam of light across the street, a road traffic accident somewhere on the one way system.

Ana's visions returned, dozens of helicopters stirred the air like a biblical storm of hornets.

The first rocket was so powerful it punched through the farmhouse wall. The second turned the stables into a fireball. The third hit a neighbour's house. The rush of air knocked Ana off her feet, burning her forehead.

Ana curled up into a tight ball on the ground and watched the earth explode beneath her feet and clods of earth thump down around her. The entire stable yard was ablaze, the horses stampeded in all directions inside a ring of fire and smoke their manes and tails alight.

The blue sky disappeared, the sun obscured by a plume of thick black acrid smoke that rose above the farm as the helicopters headed to the village.

~ ~ ~

That night Danny slept in Ana's tent. Her mattress stained black at the edges from water and earth, the duvet potmarked with mould and a coat for a pillow. All she had in the world was this tent, a pile of dirty clothes, it was heartbreaking.

"Welcome Premier Inn," she joked, picked up a can of air freshener and gave it a blast. Danny watched the spray gently settle.

"What's happen with my life?" She looked up at Danny with her grime-smudged smile, the tears welled up in her eyes, clenching her fists she had a look of anguish on her face that broke Danny's heart.

"Please you no let anyone take my baby please you find home for us no adoption please end my staying camp you and me promise." Her whole frame agitated convulsively her dark eyes darker than her ebon hair wandered in a delirium of fever her teeth chattering words gibbering breath came thick and fast.

"I promise."

"No job, no home I have nothing, just child, no person taking my son. If take him, please gun. Please you stay with my person you no leave"

"What about Yuri?"

"He no come back if come back I kill his person." Ana reached under her coat and showed Danny her flick knife.

"Why don't you go back home?" asked Danny.

"No go back home Bosnia, no more speak quiet."

"Why not? Tell me."

"Why you no go back home?" She lay back playing with the knife flicking the blade in and out.

"The war ended long ago, it's safe now."

"The war is never over, quiet please no more speak sleeping."

~ ~ ~

Ana's visions returned, they never left her for long. It was the smell she noticed first, a putrid eye watering stench. She lifted her head to find herself in a light-filled forest.

The space filled with emaciated half naked children smeared in blood and earth. They stared hollow eyed out from behind the trees like prison bars. But even in the midst of this visceral horror there is no noise. The silence is all consuming.

The blinding white forest was full of children and none of them were crying. What was the point no one would come to save them.

Among the gaggle she saw Novak his throat raw, his speech less than a croak. He coughed and dislodged something thick, bloody and black from his throat. A bullet. *"Come home."*

~ ~ ~

A reeking penetrating throat filling acrid stench clung to their clothes and hair. Danny's head just six inches from Ana's their shoulders and hips conjoined their odour entwined. Danny stunk his stomach bloated from the drink, precious little of his body was free from bites and scratches and his sores oozed pus. The flies were gathering and the wind coming from Ana was foul.

Danny's stomach runs had arrived. He didn't know how much was in his trousers, how much was in the Tesco's carrier bag at his feet or soaked through the mattress. The compulsion to drink was raw and the flies swarmed. Any movement sent the irritation of bites from ticks and ants and fleas which had set up home and laid their eggs on the sheets and the sweaty crevices of his body now racked with pain. As he could slowly feel them chewing through his stinking flesh.

In the darkest corners of the camp obscured by the shadows something malevolent crept, an evil lurked. His limbs shook and his flesh crawled and he turned as cold as stone. His heart lurched inside his chest and he could feel the acidic bile pumping from his gut to his throat as the delirium tremens took hold.

The tent was suddenly full of the sound of squeezing rodents scurrying over the pavement and Ana beside him. They were so close he could smell their sweat as they wove through the maze of their contorted bodies. Danny lay groaning rigid with shock of the unfolding horror before him. Trying to move his heels pushing at the mattress, liquid manure oozed between his fingers and rode up the small of his back but he was gripped and held fast to the sheets possessing no power of speech or movement.

Whiskers nuzzled the palms of his hands and rats buried themselves into the folds of his trousers. Danny was covered in writhing stinking shapes, a cacophony of squealing ringing in his ears lying in a puddle of faeces and bodily waste, drowning in a sea of perspiration at the limit of his emotional extremities. Black greasy mutant rats crawled over his chest sniffing at his face, a feeling of indescribable terror shook him to the recess of his soul and he screamed a silent inaudible scream. Black out.

~ ~ ~

Seven in the morning Danny went out to get some air. He reached into his pocket for his pink inhaler in case it worked. As he took it from his pocket a ten pound note inside dropped to the ground. Danny quickly went to pick it up but not quickly enough. An ogre of a man rose to his feet and strode towards him his psychotic glare unwavering fixed him in the eyes as he put his massive hands like shovels around his neck and started to squeeze.

Nausea crept against Danny's lungs, adrenaline drooled into his brain as he struggled to break free from his iron grip. Fear rose in Danny's body as the man increased the pressure around his throat choking him of breath. His heart pressing on his rib cage pounded in his ears. He reached out gasping to steal his final breaths. Whole body numb and useless he felt himself floating away from this life sinking like a stone flailing with arms of lead.

The Ogre loosened his grip, Danny gasped for oxygen backing up against the wall blood drained from his face. A fist smashed into Danny's head knocking him to the ground banging his skull against the cracked concrete path. The Ogre crouched over him trying to prise the ten pounds from his hand but Danny wouldn't let go.

The Ogre's black twisted teeth sank into Danny's neck, letting the ten pounds fall loose, he curled up into a tight ball and rolled on top of the money. Then it came to the attention of someone else. Someone small but like an angry pit-bull. Danny was squirming underneath them both like a slug as they rained down blows upon his stricken body. Punching, stamping and kicking.

The pit-bull changed tack and kicked the Ogre between the legs. The Ogre crumpled to the ground. Danny grabbed the money and rolled along the ground past them knocking over the glass bottles stacked in the alley in the frenzy.

The Ogre pulled a knife and swiped at the pit-bull cutting his jacket, he tried again the pit-bull ran. He swiped at Danny. Danny ducked, picked up a bottle and bought it down hard upon the Ogre's head. The Ogre crumpled to his knees, blood pouring from his wound. Danny sent another bottle smashing down, cracking the Ogre's skull splashing his own face with the Ogre's blood.

The Ogre keeled over holding his head, blood seeping through his fingers. His hands, jacket sleeves and shoulders now soaked red and dripping with blood as it oozed and bubbled out of his skull, pouring down his body dripping onto his boots, and soaked the pavement claret.

The Ogre unsteady on his feet staggered around, everyone stepped back. Danny was the only one left in the alley as the Ogre slumped towards him, wavered in front of him, slashing his knife around relishing the fear in Danny's eyes. Danny gasped in terror as he saw the blood soaked Ogre lumbering towards him. The Ogre grabbed him by the collar and swung him to the earth.

Pouncing upon him he swung the switch blade towards Danny's throat. Danny threw up his arms to deflect the swinging blade. The jagged edge sliced a claret streak across his knuckles and sprayed the ground.

Danny heard his heart thumping in his ears and drove the heel of his boot into the top of the Ogre's shin, the Ogre toppled over. Danny scrambled back, in a blink of an eye the Ogre was up and pounced on him again. The second swift slash flashed across Danny's face. He broke it midway with his elbow. The blade opened up his sleeve like paper, slicing his skin.

Danny grabbed the Ogre's arm and the pain was intense. Wrestling with him on the ground the Ogre passed the knife from his left to his right. Danny's heart thumped in his ears increasingly blocking out every other sound. The Ogre altered his grip thrusting the blade down towards Danny's chest. Danny kicked out with both feet knocking the Ogre off balance but the next thing he knew he was on top of him again.

Danny smashed his head into the Ogre's nose which exploded. The Ogre reeled back and Danny saw the knife in its left hand slick with his own blood and dripping to the pavement. The Ogre loomed over him glaring down at him with a face like a flesh eating zombie. Danny grabbed the arm that was holding the blade but his hands were too slippery to hold on. The Ogre plunged down and Danny felt the tip of the weapon press into the skin above his heart. The Ogre pressed his whole weight down and twisted the blade.

Danny was losing blood fast feeling his strength fading and saw the blade flash past his eyes again. Holding the Ogre's bladed wrist with his good arm he punched him with the other. The Ogre had straddled him like a pony but somehow Danny found the strength to buck him off. Kicking the Ogre in the face with both feet it crashed to the ground. Danny crawled away through the ice on hands and knees, every haggard breath a thick ragged wheeze that flared a tidal wave of pain through his burning lungs.

Still crawling through an endless debris of jagged shards of blood on glass glinting in the glow of a street lamp which doubled and blurred and started stretching away for miles. Glass cracking his knees and splintering his palms, dark shadows and distant voices incoherent nonsensical babbling and blurriness disappearing into the void.

The Ogre saw a link chain had come loose between two bollards at the foot of the alley. He grabbed the chain, looped it around Danny's neck, and started reeling him in like a fish. The links bit into Danny's neck, he tried to press his fingers underneath the noose. The Ogre wrapped another loop around his neck and pulled harder.

Danny's legs kicked out, his body shook, his heels drummed the earth in time with his heart pounding in his ears like a sledgehammer. There was a fire burning in his brain so fierce nothing could extinguish.

Lying on his back he rolled through the jagged shards of glass and trolled through the ragged shards of his life, just like the jigsaw puzzle beneath him it all came flooding back. Swamped by a tidal wave of exhaustion pulling him into a whirlpool of distorted colours and images. An all-consuming vortex sucked him under mercilessly.

Everything went black.

Danny felt the serenity of early dawn, watched the sun climb over the horizon. Saw shades of colour lift from the darkness, the red sun burning through clouds that rolled overhead.

Light shifted beneath ever changing formations of cumulonimbus and cumulus purple clouds, casting ever changing densities of sunlight and shade across the never changing landscape.

Ruminating in the undulating pasture green and thick noses buried as they chewed the cud of the lush green shoots. The half-ton patchwork black and white beasts four score and ten, with bloated udders swollen pink ,straining to drain their twenty pints of milk into a jar.

Crunching their cloven hooves through the meadow as they wobbled up the hill towards the parlour. New born calves were among the herd still covered in their sticky blanket after-birth. The cows licked the mouths of their offspring to take their first breaths, then struggled to their feet and took their first faltering steps in their short and brutal lives.

Had to be cautious when there were calves about, for these beautiful docile creatures he knew so well, could easily turn, crush him beneath their hooves, slice his skin with their horns if he threatened the new born. The mist hung low in the field, blanketed in morning dew, it felt uncomfortable with the dark hypnotic eyes of the herd upon him in one impenetrable stare as they sniffed the air and crunched the grass all around them.

Can't see, can't breathe, a light so bright spat him to the surface. Down on the ground again he saw someone standing behind the Ogre. Danny beckoned to it trying to choke out for help. Their eyes locked, he saw a flicker of recognition a glimmer of hope in his rapidly darkening existence. It stepped back and Danny saw a broken bottle in its hand. It plunged forwards. The Ogre froze its eyes wide and wild, the noose weakened around Danny's neck. The shadow stepped back, the broken bottle was no longer in its hand. The Ogre's body slumped on top of him with a jagged bottle sticking out its back, the shadow vanished.

    Sirens wailed, light flashed from emergency vehicles as they drew outside. Shimmering strobes on the gate railings, sudden torrent of electronic blue frenetic and pulsing in coalescence with the throbbing of Danny's head and heart. The whole alley flooded with blue electric light. The muffled chimes of a church bell proclaimed mortality with every passing toll. Black out.

Two silhouettes of two farm hands beyond the herd. Tried to run but his thick mud clogged boots weighed him down and slowed his stride. The restless creatures bucked and kicked their hind legs, turned and twisted on their cloven hooves. A thousand pounds of dog meat bumping and kicking out, crashing to the earth as the herd stampeded.

    Curled into a tight ball tried to protect himself, they trampled past spraying him with bovine slime. Slumped on the earth like a sack of broken bones unmoving, turning his face to the sky and looking through cow dung pupils he saw the two men towering above.

Can't see can't breathe a light so bright pulled to the surface. Bright light noise commotion chaos blood pressure heart rate increasing. Wrapped up like a kipper in a foil bag watching concerned faces peer down and ceiling strobe lights pass overhead as he's wheeled down the blue line. Black out.

Inside the old mill stood colossal bone crushing wooden cogs, stained grey from billowing clouds of flour crushed from oats in bygone days. Saw his blood dripping to the floor from his cut temple, mixing with the remnants of grey flour, turning a thick syrupy brown. His legs tied between the teeth of the giant monster started to strain and crunch at his ankles. He felt the squirming in his stomach expand and his insides ache and rock, he felt it stab, shootout stinging like acid. Ceased to be flesh instruments for torture. Did you enjoy my fear, did you salivate on the taste of my salty tear, as I screamed from the thrust of your hips? Your ragged grunts like pigs. Your noose around my throat like a hangman's rope. Tied up like a tethered goat branded like an animal. Your eyes like beasts pulverising brutalizing glazed with feral lust.

Can't see can't breathe a light so bright pushed to the surface. He awoke alone in a dark room all feeling flooded from within the punch bag he had become, he groaned.

PART TWO

Living in this brutal and savage world, gangs of addicts prowled the parks and streets at night looking for victims.

Minds destroyed by psychosis and addiction could be killed or maimed for the price of a drink. But even in the cruellest of places you could find friendships.

There was a beacon of light which hung from many a tree or lamppost, in many a hidden park or wasteland sunk deep in the city. One such beacon of light swung from the lamppost in three men's violent existence, of criminals and misfits who slept on the cold hard pavements at night.

Isaac held up his bottle of beer and watched the setting sun's rays filter through the brown glass. Watching the tiny bits of dirt and hops swirl around inside and the bubbles of gas rising to the surface of the golden brown liquid.

Casually taking a slurp and pulling a face he remarked in a hushed whisper. "Ze beer tastes much better in Czechoslovakia," but the hubbub was drowning out any audible conversation, the others hadn't heard what he said.

"Pardon?" said Earnshaw.

Isaac said it a bit louder over the drone.

"I said ze beer tastes much better in Czech-os-lov…" He realised his big mistake before he had even got the words out.

"The only fucking reason you folks are in this country is for more German Franco rule over us English."

"Who let that old cunt out?" whispered Spud. "He wants his fucking head examined."

"You're puppets of a regime you don't understand and your fate will be the Russian front."

Isaac moved closer to his friend Earnshaw and whispered, "But it's true ze beer does taste better in Czechoslovakia."

"You are a radical Jewish extremist. This country is no longer in the hands of the British and has been invaded by a subversive cult, intent on the destruction of the nation."

Earnshaw looked at Isaac as if he had two heads. "I have to admit you are right," said Earnshaw, lowering his voice. "Yes, it has come to my attention after drinking this bath water for all these years. I have to in my estimation bow to the superior quality of the Czech brewers. But under the circumstances I think you should…" Earnshaw looked at John the self-proclaimed Nazi, "…how should I put it, put a sock in it."

"The whole world is in turmoil. Nuke China, India and Lagos. Stop the immigrants or the combustion engine of our industry will fall prey to desert tribesmen intent on a reverse holocaust with a zero emissions policy."

Isaac lay on the Victorian Bandstand, a rusting relic just like himself, next to a scruffy looking stranger who had just lit up a joint. The smell is invasive, pervasive and smothering. His arthritis was playing up again, as the shock waves of pain shot from his ankles to his hips felt like he was being stabbed in the groin.

The stranger sitting next to him couldn't help noticing his grimace, so asked him about it.

"Y'alright mate?"

"Just arthritis giving me ze jip," Isaac replied then self-medicated by taking a slurp of his drink.

"You got oat for it?"

"Quack prescribed me." Isaac took a deep breath and knocked back some more of the revolting brew. Reached into his pocket and pulled out a smallish container of pills. Shaking them in the man's face he unscrewed the container, swallowed a couple of pills down with the ale.

"Does it work?"

"No."

"I could fix you up with summit better if you're interested."

"Viagra."

The stranger smiled. Isaac was amusing him.

"Seriously."

Isaac nearly choked on his last dregs of Special Brew, which tasted like the most disgusting substance ever to leave a brewery. Isaac tried to focus on the stranger, drained the bottle then gave out a belch.

"What?"

The stranger reached into his pocket and took out a little package and palmed it secretly into Isaac's hand. Isaac looked at the small packet of weed.

"Put that in your pipe and smoke it."

"What is it?"

"Pure magic, me old mam swears by it, if you like it I can get you some more. I know some bloke that grows it but I don't want everyone knowing about it." He tapped his nose. "Know what I mean."

Isaac found some filter paper and began to pack the strange looking tobacco inside, rolling it between his black stained fingers.

From where Isaac sat kneeling in the dirt of the band stand, he watched a group of four teenagers all holding on to one swing, being pushed by a couple of others. Back and forth they swung like a pendulum. The metal chains grinding and straining under their weight sounded like the metallic wheezing of a chronic asthmatic robot, groaning in time with the creaking of the overburdened seesaw. Everything needed oiling.

Kids span around and around on the roundabout then jumped off. Some falling over and some landing on both feet then staggering around like old drunks. The group of teenagers on the swing jumped off and began wrapping the swing around the overhead bar by its chains, so the little kids couldn't reach them.

In the far corner of the playground covered with ivy and brambles stood an old toilet block. As kids it was known as the gas chamber and Isaac as a child was regularly locked inside by the other kids. With a name like Zimmerman it had other evil connotations, but they never realised that at the time. If he listened hard he could still hear the ghosts of his childhood echoing in the cries and screams of the children who played now.

~ ~ ~

When the strange man entered the toilet the boy felt uncomfortable. He shuffled and moved a comfortable distance away from him and relieved himself. As the boy was urinating he noticed the man watching him. He glared back and the man looked away.

The boy was about twelve and the man had never noticed him in the park before.

"Do you want oat?"

"No," said the boy.

"You sure?"

"Yes."

The boy continued to relieve himself but the boy felt faint as the man leered at him intensely. The boy gulped as cold shivers raced up and down his spine and his whole body seemed to drain of life.

"G-g-go away." The boy stammered nervously as he pulled up his trousers. The man stood there smiling at him. The boy went to side step him but he blocked his path.

"Wh-wh-what you want?" The boy was scared, his lower lip trembling. For a few seconds the boy was paralyzed with fear and couldn't move.

The man locked the door, grabbed the boy's arms, span him around and pushed him into the cubicle. Pure unadulterated terror and fear descended.

Harder and harder deeper and deeper he stared into the eyes of the beast.

~ ~ ~

Isaac laid on his back and stared up into the cosmos, stretching back eons and eons to the dawn of time. The sky was clear under the full moon, God's creation remained in preservation for all to see.

There was a strange light in the sky that night, a giant orb glowing bright. Isaac looked at it suspended in animation before it shot across the Milky Way at the speed of light.

"Do you believe in life on other planets?" Isaac asked, no one answered. "Speak to yourself. I said do you believe in life on other planets and if so do you think might be trying to communicate with us?"

"Why would they want to talk with us?" asked Spud sitting outside his blue battered tent tickling his dog on the belly as it rolled around on the dead leaves.

"Not especially us. Intelligent life on other planets."

"Intelligent life around here, one look at him…" Earnshaw said as he motioned to John.

"With his odd shoes trousers back to front they would be back up on their ship before you could say…" Spud interjected.

"But where do they come from?" said Isaac.

"Probably some cold desolate place where light never penetrates," said Earnshaw who sat on the rust encrusted bar still methodically working on his Rubik's Cube.

"Scotland," suggested Spud.

"Why do you ask?" said Earnshaw.

"I think I just saw a flying saucer, there it was one minute zen it just disappeared, never to be seen again."

"A bit like Gold Top Milk," said Spud.

"Yes I used to love a drop of Gold Top in my tea. Zen it just disappeared"

"A bit like your flying saucer."

"Maybe ze aliens took it."

"Oh yes I like it, Intergalactic dairies now operating a giant fleet of flying saucers delivering Gold Top Milk to all four corners of the known galaxy," said Earnshaw.

"That's another thing."

"What?"

"Vell why did they name so many stars and planets after bars of chocolate?"

"What?"

"They did Mars, Galaxy, Milky…"

"The mind boggles, Mars was the God of War, oh yes I can see it now. Galileo and his ilk all gathered at the Royal Observatory. The greatest minds of millennia, all scratching their heads trying to choose between Mars Milky Way and Curly Wurly. You got it the wrong way round you idiot; they named the chocolate bars after the planets."

"All I'm saying is…"

"They may be building on the field," interrupted Spud.

"What vill happen to ze horse?"

"Send it to the knackers yard 1 suspect."

"What, that beautiful animal turned into Pedigree Chum, I won't have it I tell you, over my dead body," said Earnshaw.

"I blame ze council."

"I blame the continuation of a thousand years of Franco-German rule."

"Well yes."

"Shit stirring by world state Jewish media, Black Lives Matter, Republica, Extinction Rebellion, Just Stop Oil and yoga."

"Well yes."

"They created all of this for the Aryan race to die by evaporation due to non-breeding. The desert tribesmen behind the degeneration of the nation are forcing the natives to walk the plank of self-destruction."

"Has he taken his pills?"

~ ~ ~

He could hear a distant blues guitar rhythm as he trudged up the hill following a child in the direction of the subway. Young, innocent vulnerable he felt compelled. At the entrance to the subway stood a man rubbish blowing around his feet as he continued strumming. The music tugged at his soul. But amidst those subterranean blues that echoed down that dark gloomy tunnel, more of societies unfortunates slept and sheltered. Tugging around inside their sleeping bags, looking for some recognition and some kindly attitude from the passing crowd.

The industrial strength detergents could do nothing to mask the stench down here, as people slopped along the urine soaked floor staring down to the end of the dark passageway, where the fading light of day shone through the other side. The walls were daubed with graffiti, the roof was leaking and shouts echoed between the constant drip, drip dripping of the water and feet splashing in the puddles of the floor.

The stripped lighting along the defaced cream tiled walls kept flickering on and off where a moth fluttered. A creature of beauty with soft delicate wings of green and purple in a dark world surrounded by filth.

A woman was slumped against the wall invisible to the constant flow of human traffic, pushing and shoving as fast as they could to get out of the place. She was slurring and her words rambled along in an incoherent nonsensical babble, as she sat on a pile of cardboard with a screaming baby in her arms. The baby was shared and passed around like a parcel by others, in a grotesque game of cat and mouse to pull on the heart strings of caring but gullible passers-by. She made a fortune.

Darkness was falling as the boy walked through the deluge of flying debris washed down the tunnel by the wind. Passing the once beautiful ginger haired girl with the lesions on her face, and away from the flow of people, and away from the lost souls sitting on their blankets. Away from the hundred yards of beggars like a small community. The music still floated down with him, an edgeless volume steadily drifting in and out with the futility of existence flailing around him, and emerged from the light into the night.

The man turned right and followed the child up the main road. The music slowly fading to nothing and replaced by hydraulic fizzing pumping engine noises and calls from the street. Past streams of headlamps fog lights and sounding horns. The traffic bumper to bumper crawling at a snail's pace through the drizzle. They passed a woman in the street, a child really, saw her raise her skirt above her knickers revealing goose bumped red legs. She communicated through a car window, teeth chattering cold, she got inside and drove away.

Stepping over an old drunk passed out on the steps of the toilets the man watched the boy going inside. He followed and watched him go into a cubicle. The man waited outside for a few moments until the sweet sickly aroma of cannabis filtered under the door.

The man kicked the door open and saw him sitting on the pan smoking a joint.

"W-W-What you looking at. You wanna photo or something?" The boy choked.

"Get up."

"Why?"

"I knew you had drugs."

"Are you the police?"

"Might be."

"Please don't arrest me, it's my first time I…"

"Shut up, stand up." The boy did as he was told.

The man leered, the boy recoiled back in disgust. The boy's eyes began to water, as he stood before him a quivering, gibbering, dribbling wreck.

The man felt the power of control.

"Don't be scared don't worry."

"Please don't."

The man looked at him with disgust, pinned him against the wall, gave him a long hard psychopathic glare, put his hands around his throat and squeezed. The man started to laugh hysterically to drown out the boy's sobs. The boy cried louder and the man saw urine dribble down the boy's legs. He grabbed his arms and swung the boy hard against the wall; the boy fell and banged his head against the cistern. Dazed and confused he scrambled about on the floor, then huddled up in the corner of the cubicle.

The man thought he looked pathetic, cowering in the corner and crying like a baby. Nausea crept against the boy's lungs as he sat speechless, all feeling flooded from him as shock set in and his heart burst.

He slumped him over the toilet bowl like a rag doll.

The man was consumed by hatred. Grinding away pulverising and brutalising the poor boy. Although the man was drunk and stoned he knew what he was doing was wrong. But not even guilt or the thought of going back to prison was enough to stop him. This has nothing to do with my miserable life, he told himself. Nothing to do with the sins of my father. The fact was he liked abusing children and they enjoyed it. They were willing partners. That justified his actions in his sick and twisted illogical mind. He was consumed, unable to stop himself; he had entered his own dark fantasy and possessed the power over life and death, and revelled in his power and cruelty.

~ ~ ~

"Fuck you Mr Rubik." Earnshaw had been trying for an hour or more and so far all he could manage was one side, the orange side, the rest was a mess. John was raging at the societal machine smashing empty beer bottles at the bandstand rails. Fragments of glass everywhere his CD player pumping out obnoxious music to everyone.

"Fuck you Mr Rubik." Just as he was making progress on the green he messed up the orange again. He smashed it against the floor of the band stand and it shattered, dislodging the tiny cubes revealing the intricate inner workings and exposing how the damn thing was put together with tiny hooks and joints. On closer inspection he realised he could slot all the little cubes into each other, rebuild it from the inside out and no one would be the wiser. Earnshaw scrambled about on the ground like a dog and began to pick up all the pieces carefully minding all the smashed glass.

Spud opened up his sixth can of Tennent's Super then started to screech out the remnants of a long forgotten tune. Isaac started tapping out the rhythm on his rusty tobacco tin. Slumped next to Spud in some rolled up soiled bedding his dog began to howl. It looked like a cross between a Welsh collie and a poodle. Half its black and white coat was on the ground and strands of its coat were falling from the ends of the shears which hung loose in Spud's hand.

The dog looked pitiful as it whimpered, shook and howled at the moon.

"I want a greyhound," Spud said as a gloomy smile of desperation formed on his wrinkled face. Isaac felt the impulse to laugh but managed not to. Crouched on the ground eye level with the dog he began to mollycoddle the collie cross, patting its head and tickling its chin as it licked his face.

"I'm gonna call her Lighting Bolt she's gonna win races for me."

In the scrubland next to the playground a poor half-starved skeletal donkey with deformed hooves hobbled around. Soon the old bastard that owned the plot would shoot the donkey and sell the land to a developer for a fortune. Spud looked at the poor wretch and reminisced about his youth in Dublin. He remembered how as kids they used to race ponies across the estates and down the back streets and back alleys. It was like the Wild West back then. You could pick up an old nag for the price of a round of drinks. All over Dublin they used to roam. The only horses you found in this city were the names of pubs.

The wind began to gust lifting the dead leaves off the ground spiralling around them like twisters. The branches and twigs cracked and snapped on the fire. Spud's eyes wild and burning in the flickering flames watched dark shadows chase across the bandstand floor. Then he looked up at the stars suspended in the branches of the sycamores like lights on a giant Christmas tree, as he drank a lethal cocktail he had concocted out of an innocent looking coke bottle. He wasn't fooling anyone.

Isaac was growing ever and ever more weary with each passing second of John's behaviour. After two relentless hours of deafening music and racist ranting he finally cracked.

"Would you please turn zis music down a little?" he screamed and stood up.

"Hiel Hitler," John shouted and gave him a Nazi salute.

Earnshaw was still scrabbling about on the ground and he was incensed and faced him off. "Come on I'm itching for a fight I will kill you."

"You and whose army?" Earnshaw stood his ground. Then a bottle flew over his head crashing into the rail. Then John took another shot and the bottle whistled over his head. Soon they were coming thick and fast as John hurled missile after missile, missing Earnshaw by inches smashing and shattering into the rails and onto the bushes. Then the mad man had run out of ammunition. He leapt up screaming his lungs out and he faced Earnshaw nose to nose.

"I'm not the fucking Easter Bunny. I'm not Jesus Christ. Is this the death of humanity, cease your Islamic immoral judgemental Rasputin black magic evil ideology." Ranting in the grip of a substance induced psychotic episode all you could hear was a barrage of foul language and screaming obscenity. "You are agents, secret agents working for North Korea, China and Mongolia. All the might of Asia will descend upon us and we shall all be eating monkey brains for breakfast."

John shot out a left at Earnshaw. Earnshaw ducked and Spud was thumped on the side of the head. Spud hit back elbowing him in the face. In retaliation John grabbed Spud by the neck and pinned him up against the pillar of the bandstand.

"Whatever happens I'll have the eternal satisfaction of your mass destruction at the hands of your own ideology."

Spud grabbed his wrists, twisted him around and pulled his arms up behind his back and slammed his head into the pillar. "Bastard," said Spud. John broke free from the arm lock then Spud heard a bell ringing in his ears and in his mind was transported back forty years and visualised the bandstand transform into a smoky sweaty boxing ring of his youth. He started prancing around holding his fists up like an eighteenth century pugilist then started jabbing lefts and rights at John's head. John slumped back against the rails, in Spud's mind he could see and feel the roar of the crowd ringing out behind a thick cloud of cigarette smoke that surrounded the ring.

John tried to land a heavy right to Spud's stomach but he missed and hit the iron rail, he grabbed his fist in agony. Spud shot out a hard uppercut to his chin then a hard right then a left. John's nose exploded splattering Spud's own face, the crowd was ecstatic. John held his nose in agony blood spewing to the floor he dropped to his knees and keeled over. Earnshaw raced forward and started to count. "One two three..." John was scrabbling on the ground, "four five six." John tried to lift himself to his feet, legs weak, began wobbling in circles and crashed to the ground. "Seven eight nine..." He wasn't getting up again. "Ten." Isaac rushed towards Spud and raised his right arm in the air. The winner by a knockout.

~ ~ ~

The first thing he's aware of is the taste of salt. As the warm pungent liquid splattered his face the aroma filled his nostrils, smothering all other senses. But by the time he had spat out the salty liquid from his mouth and struggled up out of his semi coma, the fox had shot across the graveyard disappearing through a mist of freshly blown snow that whipped up across the gravestones.

The man couldn't feel his hands, his fingers had fused together and the yellow urine on his sleeping bag had frozen up in seconds. It was five degrees below zero and the dawn chorus was in full swing. All he could hear was the ceaseless chattering of starlings and he felt like his head had been squeezed in a vice. Many people have died of hypothermia sleeping rough, an old timer told him once. It felt like pins and needles all over your body, and as your core temperature drops your blood freezes in your veins, your heart slows, you can't move or talk and you die an agonizing death. In theory you could get sleeping bags that were insulated for up to minus forty, but it was still hard to stay warm. Heroin was probably the only solution for some, but in reality it only acted as a psychological barrier against the cold and you could still die of hypothermia.

The man pulled up his aching limbs and headed in the direction of the city. He trudged through the November snow past huge Celtic crosses and weather-beaten statues of angels with blackened wings and features worn away by generations of wind and rain. Past modern gravestones gleaming white with bold black lettering and older stones covered with moss. He went past the giant oak tree which stood on the centre of the cemetery black and twisted following the trail of track marks left in the snow by the fox.

Most of the graves were covered by a couple of inches of snow. The tops of vases, jam jars, small gifts and effigies were just poking through. Flowers strewn on the grave surfaces, their bright colours striking against the winter background glistening in the sun. The man heard a loud booming sound then a million starlings took flight from the bows of the old oak in a giant black cloud that screamed over his head.

He looked up at the huge war memorial which dominated the graveyard. A huge granite monolith erected in the memory of the brave men and boys who gave their lives in the two wars. Pigeons were perched on groups around the monument strutting and beating their wings, most of the plinth was covered in a thick crust of greyish green black bird droppings dried hard like glue. The man watched their piercing red eyes, their necks bobbing up and down, some with their heads tucked right inside their bodies as others hoped around aimlessly. Some missing a wing, some with one foot or one eye, some with just patches of scraggly feathers and strands of white hair sticking out. Perched precariously on the lintel.

The restless channel wind began to gust relentlessly. He needed to go, unzipped his flies and urinated over the memorial. Then just for good measure reached inside his coat pocket, withdrew his aerosol can and defaced the monument, spraying it with thick black paint across the names of the war dead. In huge black letters he wrote, 'Peter was here'.

~ ~ ~

Swirling ribbons of black starlings a million or more danced against the horizon like dark ink whirling in a jar, silhouetted against the early dawn sky. Danny watched transfixed at kidney shaped murmurations, rising and falling, tumbling, swooping and coalescing in magical synchronicity.

Danny stood at the sea edge the continuous noise of the waves lapping the shore in his ears. A loud raw as they rolled in a crackle as they recede back. The tide halfway out. The seaweed wrapped around the exposed rocks on the beach like a huge green lattice weave carpet. Where sea birds flapped squawked and pecked for food. His eyes felt sore with salt staring out across the sea to the horizon, and he could just make out the curvature of the earth. The sea looked like a grey desert of slow undulating dunes, divided into strips of black and silver shimmering bands of light. The clouds parted and the sun gently filtered through a hazy gauze of drizzle.

Danny walked further along the beach past the gushing waves scattering shells in its wake, glistening in the patches of sand revealed by the receding foam. Crab shells, limpets and sponge cast by the wind and swept across the shore.

Seagulls battled high against the darkening clouds in a wind that blew endlessly. Danny looked at the pier extending into the sea. Twenty or thirty people crammed shoulder to shoulder to dangle a string of bait over the edge into the swell, waiting endlessly until a dark shadow appeared just below the surface of the water, moving ever so closely towards them like a giant oil slick. But it was alive as suddenly the surface started to bubble and silver shapes burst to the surface.

The cold took hold and Danny started to shiver. He sat down behind a breakwater covered in a thick green carpet, and encrusted with limpet shells and draped with a curtain of black seaweed for protection from the elements.

He watched two men trudge up the thick green mossy carpet towards a small decrepit weather beaten boat near the sea edge. They hauled the boat across the shingle uncomfortably and into the sea, they jumped in, got struck by an incoming wave. The wave lifted up the end of the boat and foam encased them, as they jostled about scraping the sea bed they pushed out with the oars. The little vessel buffeted up and down on the swell viciously and they tasted the salty spray. The dark clouds parted and they were struck by a shaft of sunlight that shot from the heavens and were bathed in golden rays. Painting the sea turquoise and shading the breakwater in a purple haze. Danny watched a boy by the sea edge unwind an orange string from an H reel and slowly let it settle beneath the waves, his hook baited with bacon rind and it slowly floated down to the rocky crevasse where the crabs gathered.

Memories returned.

Limbs jerk stomach turns throat clenches. Pain washes through him like the waves crashing to shore. Panting and flaring with the rhythm of the sea. Cries smothered by the screeches of seagull wails.

Just like a stricken vessel left smashed against the rocks after a storm he lay marooned on the shore.

Snapped mast, bent sail, soul worn frail.

The pain still burns like a fire. Nothing will extinguish or erase the memory of your wake. The scars I bear are a constant reminder of you.

It was a bitter dawn, bereft of joy, bereft of hope, bereft of spirit. The freezing mist was rolling in again, drifting through the shadows and curling through the air. Over parked cars, street signs and benches, creating strange ghost-like apparitions.

A beautiful russet fox in its thick winter coat, caught in the glow of a street lamp, crouched low shrouded in mist unperturbed. Transfixed, it seemed to yawn, exposing its sharp fanged teeth as a gust of wind ruffled the hair on its back, before disappearing through a gap in a torn wire fence.

Padding through the condemned housing estate, it had to run the gauntlet. Past drunks and junkies on both sides of the street. Not many people lived here anymore except a few squatters. The streets were filthy as were the people and there were burnt out cars on the grass verges. Walls awash with graffiti most of the windows and doors either smashed or boarded up. But there were no rats simply because rats demanded a higher standard of living.

Padding around the back of the block past a mountain of old mattresses, fridges, washing machines and all manner of broken household furniture, the fox passed a low loader backing up to the edge of the pile. Lifting its tail gate a waterfall of white goods cascaded into the stream of waste.

Padding further down a narrow alley past crumbling storage sheds the fox came sniffing towards Danny, crashed out in the empty shell of a building next to a wheelie bin. The fox started clawing at the dustbin, pulling it down it spilt the contents to the earth. Burying its head deep inside the bin it began to claw great lumps of rubbish under its legs. Danny was getting pelted in his sleep as it dug. It stopped digging and started sniffing at the ground, then climbed back inside the bin. Half its body disappearing inside a plastic drum it clawed deeper and deeper into the waste. Empty cans, ready meal packets and empty pizza boxes flying everywhere. Danny awoke and was trying to shield himself as much as possible as bits of rancid pasta and fried rice got in his eyes and mouth. Trying to spit it out the fox stopped digging. Slowly twisting his head around he saw the creature of the nights narrow dark eyes all sensing, its nose wrinkled. Curling up its mouth exposing its fangs thick with dripping drool it lurched forwards.

Noses inches apart, it fixed him in the eyes. Danny froze with panic as his pulse thumped hard in his head he flinched as the fox snarled and screeched then sank its massive jaws into the side of his leg. Danny felt its jaws slowly puncture the skin around his thigh. The increasing bite pressure slowly penetrated his grey tracksuit bottoms piercing the flesh underneath. Danny saw patches of blood slowly seep through the cotton. Caught in a vice-like grip digging its jaws in deeper its claws scratching at his knees it latched on.

As quick as a flash Danny pressed down hard on the top of its head, it snapped at his fingers ripping at his knuckles. Danny managed to kick it off and snapping at a chicken carcass it ran away.

~ ~ ~

Danny seemed to be in a squat; he froze as he heard voices and the sound of smashing glass. He jumped as he saw two women emerge from an open door. He knew they weren't twins, he was just seeing double. Wind chimes chattered as the morning breeze wandered through the open door. Inside the shell of the building one of the walls had been smashed through. He could see people lying on a threadbare carpet and on soiled mattresses surrounded by filth. Some were laying in a foetal position groaning loudly, one had a needle sticking out of his arm and another had a tourniquet wrapped around his thigh and was slapping his groin red raw looking for a vein. Danny didn't feel safe. He had heard all the rumours about this place, about the whores and their twisted appetites, about people asphyxiating to death during sado-masochistic sex games. He grabbed his gear and hit the street.

There were no flowers blooming between the cracks of the cold hard pavements. Just the haunting echoes of friends long dead carrying on the wind. Danny was desperate for a drink but had no money. He had no option left except to humiliate himself through begging on the street. Occasional do-gooders would talk to him, give him advice, tell him about their lives, tell him to sort himself out, to get a job. But the words they spoke were as helpful as the wind they farted. Some people had an incredible facility for argument. But the art of talking wasn't dead with some nor was the art of debate. Sat on a pavement outside a television show room sitting in front of a fifty inch widescreen, magnetic forces interrupting and merging news of the view and views of the news, passing cars ruining the picture. But most of it was worthless words; words can't pay for food or drink.

The wheels of cars spewed dirty sludge from under their tyres splashing. The words of men ground him down and crushed him. But this is what happens to people who choose to beg on the city streets among people of infinite ignorance and wickedness.

Trudging determinedly weaving his way through the impossible movement of human traffic, noise echoing around him was disorientating. It was hard to navigate through the hordes. All Life was here, the legless, the armless, drug addled people rubbing shoulders with the shoppers on a Sunday afternoon. Danny passed a child struggling to push her disabled mother up a steep incline. A man in a wheelchair with hands for arms and one leg with a hideous claw for a foot. A blonde woman screaming among the continuous stream of people flowing like a great river through a gorge of stores.

Danny walked past a grubby twisted creature, more like a wild animal than a human being, hunchbacked and hunched over searching through the rubbish bins and poking in the ashtrays for dog ends. There was a group of people huddled together on some steps singing and pushing each other around to the sound of an old radio. They didn't care how much noise they made as long as they couldn't hear the thoughts in their own heads. Tramping through the streets there were people in every doorway collecting change in hats and cups slowly drowning in slurps of cheap vodka.

Danny saw a crushed up man with a crushed up beer can in his hand sitting on a cracked pavement slab, with all manner of filth being blown over his body. He didn't seem to know or care, screaming, "Fuck you all… fuck you all." Further down a man hobbled towards him on a pair of crutches and a bandage around his head. A yellow McDonald's balloon gently floated in front of him, he stamped on it hard. It sounded like a bomb exploding. Sound waves vibrating and bouncing off all the buildings.

Icy blasts of wind coming off the sea started screaming in Danny's face. Passing MacDonald's transvestites paraded in tight fitting blouses and fishnet tights stomping around cat calling, cackling, propositioning old men for kicks. Screeching out relentlessly like alley cats. Groups of kids pushing each other around, scuffles breaking out between rival packs, mobile glued to their faces, dropping drink cans, crisp packets and farts. Disabled, disfigured, mentally unstable drunks on mobility scooters. A dozen foreign languages, day trippers piling off coaches the streets awash with cigarette butts, a few pennies but Danny's on the constant look out for that elusive fiver. Dogs barking kids screaming parents yelling dog piss running down the cracks in the pavement.

But all she heard was the voices of angels in her head above the chaos. As she stood at her alter a rusty green metal BT electrical box draped with a blue velvet cloth. Adorned with a jam jar of flowers and a picture of the Messiah, a bible in one hand a wooden staff in the other dressed in a purple cloak she quoted from the gospels. "The Lord says these are the last days prepare yourself for the reckoning yet to come."

An eye watering malodorous stench winded its way towards Danny in the shape of a woman, wheeling a shopping trolley of rags and rubbish through the hordes. Her hair painted white she wore a face of clown's makeup. It spooked him.

~ ~ ~

The Our Lady of the Immaculate Conception and Saint Peter in Chains, Strict Baptist Chapel, had a sign which stretched as far as the street itself. Spencer sat down in the small cramped office space surrounded by shelves full of binders and reports. He was clutching hold of his portfolio like his life depended upon it. He had outlined his proposal to Kenny the shelter manager who sat stone faced throughout his pitch. He tried to look interested but he had more pressing matters to think about.

Spencer showed off his glossy black and white prints of various depressed parks full of depressed looking people, sitting on park benches. People in various states of inebriation laughing, smiling, pulling faces and giving two fingers to the camera. Old grainy atmospheric shots of men bedded down in shop doorways as men in business suits and children walk by. Old men with wrinkled faces stroking their dogs. He boasted of his art exhibition he had taken all over the country and his plans for an installation at the local library later in the year, and all the money he had raised for charities like Crisis at Christmas and Shelter. He even showed him a photograph of himself standing outside Buckingham Palace presenting a cheque to the Duke of Sussex with a smug grin on his face. He was working on a book, a photographic journal to be more precise and was asking permission to take some pictures of the centre and some of the clientele to publish within. He wanted to accompany the night outreach team to various locations to document the local wildlife.

Kenny warned him of the dangers, he explained that a lot of people didn't like having their photos taken. Someone poking a camera in their face. Spencer assured Kenny he would ask their permission first and would treat the whole exercise with the utmost anonymity and respect.

"I assure you Kenny I only have their best interests at heart. I would do nothing to jeopardize that."

"I will ask on your behalf but don't go walking around at night by yourself and don't approach any large groups in the park, it's not advisable."

Inside the woman who helped run the centre shuffled about with her creaking bones and arthritic legs serving tea and breakfast. Danny went up to the counter and tried to focus on the sign behind her.

'Donations gratefully received'. Danny still possessed a modicum of self-respect. He checked the contents of his pockets and with his blood stained fingers put the dried blood encrusted coins on the counter. She thought Danny seemed to be in some kind of trance; she deposited the money in the till before pouring out the dark liquid tea into a cracked mug. The four rotating objects behind her said it was eleven o'clock. Danny had somehow been rocketed four hours into the future in a matter of minutes, another blackout. The glass window of the time machine had descended between him and the bustling crowd; nothing seemed real, nothing mattered, he was in complete oblivion.

Danny sat opposite an odorous stranger with two blurring heads. Danny offered his hand and he didn't shake it. The stranger looked at him with contemptuous superiority with his black eye and squashed nose.

"What happened to you?" Danny asked.

"Midnight knock at door beaten up by police for nowt. Kidnapped false imprisonment sent to high security gulag, medieval psychological and physical torture cloggins still at large."

"Sorry I asked."

"George Floyd world-wide media event. Me tortured to within an inch of my life no media response. Why?"

Danny shrugged.

"Fuck off you southern bastard," he replied blasting Danny with his paint stripper breath. The glass window of oblivion was no barrier against the insult, the words crushed his whole happy illusion to shreds. He got up moving through the heaving mass of bodies he sat next to another man slurping from his soup with snot hanging from his nose. More people came shuffling through the door like a long line of sherpers carrying everything they owned on their backs, eyes watering from the cold and empty bellies. Danny got out his phone and showed him a picture of a man. "Do you know this person?" Danny asked. The man wiped the snot from his nose and grabbed the phone pulling a face he shook his head and handed it back to Danny covered in a film of green slime. He wiped it on his trousers.

Wiping his chin the stranger said. "Looks like a shape shifter."

"What?"

"Annunci."

"Annunci?"

"Sssssh." He looked around nervously. "They drink human blood to look like us." Leaning forward in Danny's face he continued in a hushed voice. "Half human half alien creatures who have infiltrated the planet." He checked around again for anyone listening. "Lizard people."

Danny went to move but he grabbed his arm. "Annunci blood drinking flesh eating shapeshifting extra-terrestrials who want to take over the planet." Danny tried to move but he grabbed his arm tighter to the table and glared at him in the eyes trapped. "They have controlled us since the dawn of time, the sons of Anu."

"Anu?"

"Annunci are the sons of Anu who came from a distant galaxy." He kept staring at Danny with his yellow eyes. "They travelled across the depths of time and space until they reached earth and created man from the mud of the earth."

"Where did they come from?" Danny felt he had to humour him.

"They came from Nibiru. It's two hundred million light years from earth."

So are you Danny thought.

More people started piling through the door out of the cold with flushed cheeks, watery eyes and empty bellies and found a seat. They were serving all day breakfasts. Plates piled high with sausage egg bacon beans and mushrooms. The gorgeous smell filled the room and steam from plates curled high into the ceiling then dissipated. All consuming smells imbued his senses like a morphine hit, just better. Plates started to be passed around and people began stuffing their faces. A long queue formed as the volunteers in the kitchen started shouting out orders. "More eggs more bacon more toast." Some of the orders were lost in translation so people started to do mimes. Romanians clucked like chickens for eggs, grunting like pigs for bacon, but no one seemed to know how to make a noise like a mushroom.

There had to be at least sixty people inside. Rucksacks, blankets and sleeping bags strewn everywhere against the walls and piling up on top of one another. The air was thick with foreign tongues all merging together to create one massive wall of sound. The lizard man got up to get his breakfast. Danny made good his escape.

Earnshaw was sitting in the corner talking with Isaac. "From now on I will never drink coffee at Costa's again," announced Isaac.

"Why?"

"They found shit in it."

"What?"

"Human faeces, was in the paper Nero, Costa and Starbucks. They did tests and found traces of human faeces urine and semen in ze coffee and ze tea. They weren't washing their hands properly."

"We've already swallowed a ton of shit. It makes as much difference as a canary pissing in the Atlantic," said Spud.

"Oh it can, you only need a microscopic amount and you can catch hepatitis and if you catch that you've got a seventy percent chance of kicking the bucket," said Earnshaw.

"Unlikely," said Spud.

"I used to work in microbiology and I am telling you. You only need five millilitres in a litre of blood before you're sick."

"Yes," Isaac agreed, "and bacteria multiplies, it spreads fast in ze human body."

"It's an aggressive agent kills all defence molecules it's not worth the risk."

"How do you know?" said Spud.

"How do I know my dear fellow? There are highly sensitive precision measuring devices but I wouldn't expect you to understand the complexities of the apparatus. Suffice to say they could be lethal in the wrong hands."

"I'm not an idiot you know."

"You don't know a single thing about the basic rudimentary principles of chemistry."

"How do you know?"

"The idea is preposterous that you two country bumpkins with limited education would possess the brain capacity and technical knowledge to understand instruments of such complexities."

"Paradoxically ze most expensive coffee in the world is full of excrement made from it."

"Made from shit?" asked Spud.

"Not human shit. Civet shit," said Isaac.

"What's a civet?"

"What's a civet?" Earnshaw raised his eyes in despair.

"It's an animal a bit like a polecat that lives in Indonesia eats the coffee beans and shits them out. Farmers turn it into coffee. Costs a fortune," Isaac answered.

Isaac saw Aaron walk in the door and slowly strolled up towards them. He placed his massive hands like shovels on Earnshaw's shoulders. He looked even bigger closer up with his head full of scars and Leeds United tattoo burned into the side of his scalp.

"How do Professor."

Earnshaw turned around and faced him squarely in the chest.

"How do A-A-Aaron." Aaron slammed a copy of the local rag down on the table rattling the cups and plates.

"That fuckin nonce from't paper."

"Err, I don't know what you're talking about," replied Earnshaw.

"Thy knows that kiddy fiddler friend of yours."

Earnshaw was still none the wiser. Aaron towered over him and slapped him round the face quite hard. "Ask yer sen one question, Professor, that was the left." He grabbed him by the collar, he raised his hand flexing his massive digits before him forming a fist. "That were left this is the right, this'l kill thee, make myself clear, that kiddy fiddler from't paper your mucker I've seen all of thee together up bandstand. All three peas int' pod sitting ont' bandstand watching the little kiddy-winks. I bet your pockets are full of smarties, stay away from't park if I see thee any of thee i'nt park from now on you're dead."

Danny picked up a copy of the local rag and saw the picture on the front page. It was like being hit by a freight train his whole body convulsed and went into meltdown blubbering and shuddering.

~ ~ ~

Only the breeze in the foliage and the rustling of unseen creatures in the thicket accompanied the noise of his own rasping breath. Punctuated occasionally by the barking of dogs and his rapidly increasing heartbeat, instinctively aware of the possible risk of attack from people that lurked in the bushes.

Carefully Isaac stepped through the twisted and stunted trees, picking his way through the detritus of the springy mossy floor. Grey mist hung all around him creeping through the trees and around his knees in ever changing folds. It seemed like a long way to go for a quick slash but the toilets were a crime scene and had been taped off. Forensics was snooping around looking for blood splatter under infrared lights.

The thicket grew over an abandoned graveyard, blocks of marble and stone protruded from the ground covered in a decaying overcoat of lichen and parasitic mould. Ferns and creeping plants rose from the damp earth like thorny vipers wrapping themselves around the limbs and strangling the necks of angels, and cherubs with broken wings laid split and submerged beneath the undergrowth. Isaac's feet got caught in the vines like trip wires and he was trapped like a rabbit in the snare. He tried to extradite himself from the spot but he was rooted to the spot. Unscrewing a bottle of scotch he drank in the liquid and the silence of the woods.

There was a stirring among the boughs sending a dismal melancholic whisper through the trees. Looking into the deeper recess of the thicket he had to catch his breath. An angel covered in thick undergrowth wings stretched, arms reaching out beckoning to him in a posture of despair. Black crows with a vivid blue sheen reflected in the moonlight hovered and dipped in the canopy above his head. Their calls overflowed from the tented depths of the thicket as they took to flight and circled above him. He looked up into the sky of jagged clouds then down again.

A woman in white stood before him swathed in a burial cloth, a phosphorus glow emanated from her. Head bowed a thick mass of tangled black hair fell across her face. The trees seemed to rotate all around him; the woods were filled with crying laughing voices the angels gathered surrounding him in the Dell. The whole thicket began to spin around and around dizzyingly, he felt hands reaching out grabbing at his arms and legs the entire wood revolving cries reverberating then everything stopped.

Between midnight and early dawn the heavy tempest drops hammered hard upon the roof of the bandstand. The storm thundered and raged above them. Rain turned to hail whirling wildly in the cutting wind.

Isaac saw a curious nebulous light that hung like a milky blur against the gloom of the sky. Slowly drawing energy from the electrically charged air then it faded and was gone only to reappear in a heartbeat like a flickering light bulb pulsating white and green and growing in intensity.

Had the spook followed him back from the thicket seeking attachment?

In the dark between the flashes of lightning the luminous figure was clearly visible and it seemed incredible to Isaac that the others hadn't seen it. The apparition shook with an agitation and filled the bandstand with its glow, vibrating and swelling feeding off the electricity of the storm. It began to float in the air and moved towards him, he faintly discerned a face and the outline of a human form.

His heartbeat increased, his limbs quivered and his eyes bulged with terror. Earnshaw stood up and stared at him. Isaac, frozen with fear, tried to speak. The ghost raised its head from its droop and glared through a pair of black eyes at him its face withered wholly malign with evil intent that foamed and frothed with unimaginable evil beaming from its black leering eyes. A curdling hissing sound spewed from her demon lips.

Isaac's arms went limp, his body convulsed, his head dropped to one side drooling from his mouth. Earnshaw shook him.

"Come on, we have to go" he said.

"Leave him, he's drunk."

They gathered up their belongings and left him as the clouds clashed together thunderously at war. Isaac was no more.

PART THREE

That morning Ana was stood by the Clock Tower hassling people for money near the Halifax cash point. She was agitated. She always dressed smart. You could pick up some classy outfits from the Salvation Army for a pound and all the toast you could eat for free.

Chilean buskers were playing pan pipes in native South American dress with eagle feathers in their hair. A hypnotic melody which summoned up an image of a cold Pacific breeze blowing across the Andes and a herd of a thousand lamas. A surreal juxtaposition if ever there was one as prolific shoplifters in puffer jackets with holes in the lining prowled market stalls.

Ana used to shoplift and she had slept on the blue mattress a few times. But these days she could make far more money far quicker far easier by using her killer looks and feminine charms. Flirting and cosying up to lonely old men who would give her half their pension money for some much needed attractive female companionship. There weren't many of them left she hadn't got her claws into.

Danny arranged to meet Ana at the takeaway. It was warm inside and his clothes were sticking to him. They both removed their coats, underneath she was dressed in a tight fitting yellow dress with too much flesh on show.

"You eat. Just quick smoke," she said and popped outside. It wasn't busy inside the takeaway, there were lots of empty tables and chairs. One lad with a pizza face was busy mopping the floor while he chatted to his female colleague who was busy cleaning tables. He was complaining about the manager who didn't give him the Saturday off to watch the football. She told him that football was a stupid game and that real men played rugby.

Danny sat and watched Ana through the glass door. "Five minutes!" she shouted. One minute and she was off, shouting at people across the street shit head this and shit head that. She threw the fag butt on the ground and came back in, sat next to Danny. A stranger sitting in the corner minding his own business caught her eye, she winked at him.

"This man FBI," she said, got out her phone and began scrolling through giving the man sneaky glances. She leant forward to Danny and whispered. "You see this man blue shirt tattoo on neck keeps looking me. I remember where I see him before he body guard Prince Harry." She lowered her voice and looked at Danny in a trance. "What if it him what if he the man makes phone calls no one answer mystery number?" She showed Danny her phone, flicked through her call history. "Here this one number call me six times no one speak I get text another one time it say I have pictures of you and Harry. Paparazzi. Maybe he find out about me Prince Harry hotel London maybe sell newspapers."

She showed Danny a picture of Harry and Meghan on her phone. She claimed she knew him, she claimed they had a secret relationship and she claimed her unborn child was his.

"What if he find out about our baby what if Prince Harry want baby?"

"Really?"

"Yes I no lie" She put her bag on the table and started to sort through it, makeup, documents from probation and mental health social services, until she found her cigarettes and ran out for another smoke.

The radio was playing in the takeaway, it was the eight o'clock news bulletin. The main headline was about a man that got stabbed to death by his mentally ill girlfriend during a psychotic episode. She had a chronic addiction to synthetic cannabis and was suffering from substance abuse schizophrenia. The man in the corner got up to leave staggering under the weight of his heavy rucksack as Ana came back in. She screamed, "This man terrorist you no take my son Prince Harry."

Everyone stood and stared. Danny just ignored her then like a flick of a switch she was calm again. Danny sat drinking his Coca-Cola thinking about that woman that stabbed her boyfriend.

"Buy chicken bucket I wait for you outside," Ana demanded. "Just quick smoke." Danny went up to the counter and ordered. Through the window he could see her smoking again and having an animated conversation with some down and out, then she gave him a big kiss and a hug. After a few minutes the girl gave him the chicken bucket and he went outside. A man sat in the doorway shaking as he gulped vodka.

"Danny please chicken please very much." Danny passed her the bucket, she then gave two drumsticks to the man and kissed him.

They hit the street and so began a never ending succession of hugging kissing and chicken handouts. You couldn't move for rough sleepers and buskers and chuggers. Some buskers were good, some horrendous playing everything from Mozart on violins to Motor Head on traffic cones. A man shuffled past them blown out of his head on something. As they continued down the street the wind blew harder, there was a significant police presence.

Many times the crowd had to part to let them through. "Heroin shit heads," Ana screamed the man ignored her. More down and outs shuffled past like the night of the living dead, an endless rallying cry of "Heroin shit heads," and more chicken handouts. A couple were having a loud domestic outside Mc Donald's. The woman got up abruptly from her seat, tipped the table over and the coffee flew. She picked up the chair and it flew crashing into the bin. The whole crowd slowly pushed back. A big security guard pushed himself through the rabble and made a grab for the woman pushing her against the wall. Her fella was up like a shot trying to pull him off her when another guard ran out and tried to pull him off his colleague. He got his arm behind the man's back and forced him to the earth. A third came running, then without warning Ana jumped on his back, he twisted her around and around until she fell off, grabbed her and started dragging her across the pavement yelling and cursing while his mate was sitting on the boyfriend slowly squeezing the air out of his lungs.

Two dark figures came running along the square, a police four by four swung round the corner, snow and ice spewing out from under its tyres. Followed by a panda car the four by four braked and skidded to a halt. Two policemen jumped out and pulled Tasers, another two jumped out the panda and tried to break up the fight. In the struggle Ana hit a policeman still kicking and screaming and flinging her arms about they managed to drag her off. They closed in on her pointing Tasers screaming at her to stay down. Danny foolishly tried to intervene, two people grabbed his arms and started dragging him along the crowded pavement while being kicked and spat on by the football supporters. Legs were coming from all directions, as they cheered and hollered before he was hoisted up and pushed over. His legs buckled beneath him and he fell down into a puddle of slush. People stepped over him, the only help he received was a kick to the ribs. He tried to stand but slipped and banged his head on the curb. He could see Ana being hoisted up off the ground. In the melee they held her down on the bonnet and tied her wrists with cable ties.

A riot van jostled through the crowded street surrounded by a pandemonium of yobs, who hammered and kicked and tried to rock the vehicle. The police jumped out and started chucking people in the back Ana included. Danny lay on the ground shivering dazed. Then the heavens opened up a deluge upon him and he saw the police van drive away.

~ ~ ~

The following day a police car drove through a puddle of slush and grit which spewed out from underneath the tyres, and splattered thick muddy flakes of brown ice along the pavement edge and the bottom of Danny's sleeping bag. When the traffic lights on the road works changed to red the cars grinded to a halt. The policeman lowered the car window and shouted across to Danny sat on the street.

"Afternoon." The outside temperature was dipping as late afternoon approached but the policemen were warm and comfortable inside the luxurious leather interior of the Impreza. He started singing very loudly and very badly. "We are the champions, we are the champions. You watch the game?"

"No," said Danny.

"Your girlfriend got very carried away last night biting and kicking everyone, had to let her cool off in the cells last night. Let her out when she calmed down."

"She ain't my girl."

"Whatever."

"She's schizo," said the driver.

"What?" shouted Danny over the traffic noise.

"Bipolar. BPD one or the other nuts basically. The drugs have fucked her brains up. Psychotic dude." He lit up a cigarette and blew the smoke out the window. "She's using you. She uses everyone. She's figured out a way of doing it and she's good at it. You can't help her don't bother trying. She's mugging you off she don't give a fuck about anyone except herself."

"She might get better," said Danny. The constable creased up in a wheezing chuckle coughing on the cigarette.

"Take my advice, keep away from her she's bad news you know it anyway." The lights changed and the car jerked forwards.

Moments later Danny saw her staggering down the main road towards him. She had a bump on her head and the right side of her cheek had swollen up a black eye and blood on her teeth.

"Fucking hell what happened?"

"People punch me. Not my fault why people punch me I good person."

"Did you punch them first?"

"Maybe."

"You have to be careful."

"Huh, be careful this all you say."

"You're an intelligent person, a good person, change or you get deported."

"No deported council give me home. Maybe London. Stupid council why not here?"

"London's not far."

"I want to live here not London."

"You can't turn down the offer they're trying to help you. Do you want to be on the streets forever?"

Sometimes it was like her entire personality transformed in a second, her looks her demeanour her entire being in a flash. She stood in front of Danny screaming like the wind in his face stamping up and down like a child hot with sweat wild eyed with fury.

"What you say shit head, what is this bullshit? I kill you I promise you dead." Then she turned around.

"Where are you going?" Danny asked. Like a flick of a switch she was calm again.

"I go speak Andy."

"Who's Andy?"

"This person like witch doctor herbalist, he give me medicine for pain for relax woman pregnant. Andy says I can sleep with him no sex just sleeping."

The roads were freezing over and the council had been putting down grit all day. Trickles of water were running down the piles of slush and encroaching him. Ana walked off passing Kenny walking towards him in the opposite direction.

"How's Ana?" he asked.

"Ok."

"Ok. She looked a bit pissed off, maybe she needs a morphine shot."

"She doesn't, does she?" Danny looked disturbed. Kenny sensed he was troubled. Danny didn't say a word he didn't have to Kenny knew his bones and the calcium and blood that swam around his veins, he was just the same once.

"Someone's got to help her, everyone else has given up," said Danny.

"There's a good reason for that."

"She's a good person, she's just gone off the rails a bit."

"She's sick."

"She could get better again."

"You can't change people, you can't make her better, no one can fix her, she can only fix herself you know that."

"I know."

A member of the public threw a few coppers into his collection pot.

"You have to stop picking her up all the time you have to let people crumble before. Look I know it's hard but you're taking on hell walk away while you still can it's out of your control. You can't do anything. She will destroy you, she will suck you down with her and you will both be dead. Trust me, it's easier for her to drag you down to her level than to rise to yours."

"I won't give up."

"I lived with an addict for years. I loved her more than anyone before or since, I didn't even smoke or drink back then. Had a good job and a decent flat. Two years later I was living in a tent and pissing in a coke bottle. I had to walk away otherwise I was going to die and yes I still love her miss her but I love being alive more, you're better off without her"

"I'm not."

"Why is it more about you than her?"

"Don't psychoanalyse me."

"I'm not take a good look at yourself, think about it, and examine your motives honestly."

~ ~ ~

Danny headed to the park. Eight o'clock and it's chucking out time at the homeless centre. Soon he would see them all shuffling and staggering through, the dealers won't be far behind in fact they are already here. Drugs are sold, bought and smoked openly in this park. It suffers from its location slap bang between the homeless shelter, the prison and the mental hospital. Subsequently it is a magnet for every addict, every dealer and every fruit loop in the city. Now the gangs are flooding in from London on the county lines, taking advantage of the less sophisticated crack-downs in the capital. There's a lot of fighting in this park, so many feuds, a few murders even all drug related. It's a shame the park looks so nice with its manicured lawns, flower beds, fountains, statues and tree lined avenues.

A large group had gathered in the park, Danny could hear shouting, swearing and barking dogs. There were ten of them in all swaggering through shoving and intimidating people who got in their way. Danny was no stranger to rough looking mobs but they took the biscuit. Scars on their heads and fists, teardrop tattoos pouring down their faces. Swigging from vodka bottles then without hesitation slinging them over their shoulders to smash to a million pieces. Aaron was head of the group dressed in a white vest and cap. Whatever the weather he had a nasty reputation for violence, people knew to keep their distance, no such chance for Danny as the group surrounded him.

"How do, we're looking for Mohammed seen oat of him?" said Aaron towering over Danny.

"A few days ago, why?"

"We want a quiet word with him."

"He might ask why?"

"Okay we don't like other people selling their shit in't park. The park belongs to us."

"Right did you buy it off the council?"

Aaron looked at the others sniggering and looked back at Danny and grinned.

"You're a funny man," he said.

"Seen Ana?" Danny asked him.

"No."

"Did you give her anything?" More sniggering emanated from the crew.

"What's it to you?"

"She's about to drop."

Aaron placed his massive hands on Danny's shoulders. They just stared then.

Danny said, "Go fuck yourself Aaron."

Aaron's eyes flickered in astonishment then grinned. Danny realised his mistake he felt paralysis stricken, his nose met Aaron's head. He heard a crack then felt immense pain. Everything imploded the next thing he knew he was lying on the grass and they were all standing over him looking down.

"By rights I should kill thee I've my reputation to consider. You're a funny bugger but I like you." They left him sprawled out on the earth.

Danny staggered into the toilets dripping blood along the floor he saw his reflection in the cracked mirror, bloodshot tired eyes set in a pale ghost like face. A mass of cuts and grazes and a swollen bloody nose that wouldn't stop bleeding. Danny went into a cubicle and span around the confined space dazed, confused and disoriented, unable to coordinate his movements. Black out.

Danny feared the darkness for he thought that the devil was on his track. But as long as he stayed here it couldn't touch him. Head resting on the edge of a cracked toilet seat, the halogen bulb dim but still flickered and burned from the ceiling above his head. Hugging the lavatory bowl full to the rim with diarrhoea Danny shook as he felt the dark presence close around him. Saturating the air heavy and oppressive emanating an odour of corruption and decay, it slowly sucked the light from the room.

Maligned forces slathered over the cold tiled floor like giant black slugs towards him. Dark incantations known to few oozed up in his diseased imagination gaped, wailed and banged against the cubicle door. Danny, a quivering gibbering wreck of disordered nerves, a discombobulated rhythm of movement gave way to spasmodic convulsions. Banging banging on the door. Blackout.

~ ~ ~

Sometime later he regained consciousness. He eventually sat down on the pan, blood still dripping profusely listening to the cistern's flush and drip. He grabbed some paper from the roll and painfully blotted up his nostrils, he opened the door and fell outside. Using the sinks for leverage he pulled himself off the floor but his hands slipped and he fell onto the waste paper bin. He tried again holding onto the sink and walls for leverage until he found the door and hobbled in the direction of the town.

Bleary-eyed and puffy faced he held on to the road bridge rails for support as cars and lorries thundered beneath him. He went around the back of Morrisons supermarket. A lot of rough sleepers liked to loiter around it. There was a small labyrinth of alleyways and bin yards where the store regularly threw out food waste, uncontaminated sandwiches and cakes just past the best before date. This was a safe and secluded place with an amalgamation of small brick alcoves just big enough for someone to bed down for the night. If you didn't sleep in a tent in the woods it was advisable to stay in small groups near security cameras for safety reasons. It could be dangerous if you were on your own, you could become an easy target for a group of drunks who might try to attack you or slash all over you while asleep.

Danny wanted a moment of clear thought away from the constant fears playing in his head. Then he saw her from a distance slumped by a cash point invisible to the queue of people. Senseless but stunning that was his image of her dressed in blue torn clothes and one shoe with a dreamless expression and grime smudged smile sitting on a pile of cardboard in the drizzle.

"You okay?" she slurred. Then tears welled up in her eyes. "This shit situation no like live on the streets too much dangerous," she said.

"You like dangerous."

"Not anymore."

"How about the accommodation?"

"No accommodation."

"I don't understand why they don't help you're pregnant."

"I know stupid council they promise me what. I have baby in tent. You speak with probation maybe better no time no nappies no powder no cosmetic for baby Jesus fuck sake no more children no more pregnant why I not kill this child. This man Andy give me ecstasy now these problems."

"What about Andy?"

"I was stay with Andy no like Andy anymore he say please Ana sex all the time. But me no bitchy slag whore he old man he try to fuck me I kick him hard in bollocks he no try again. I run away lose shoe. I disgusting bad mother I know, you smoke with me?" Ana unzipped her bag and rolled a joint. "You smoke with me?"

Danny said nothing.

"You smoke with me?"

"No."

"Why not you my friend?"

"Of course I am."

"You hurt you nose you need go hospital."

"Aaron Bickerdyke."

"Aaron Bigger dick."

"Yes."

"One second I go toilet." Ana squatted and Danny smelt a pungent odour and watched the ground beneath her feet flood with hot yellow steaming liquid, Danny put his head in his hands.

"Go night shelter," she said, wiping her tears.

~ ~ ~

Kenny found a heroin wrap in the toilets and as a result gathered everyone together and laid down the law. Everyone had to be interrogated about it but nobody was going to grass. He made the rules and he ran this place with a rod of iron, he had to.

The dog John Joe was holding started to snarl curling up the sides of its cheeks and exposing its nasty incisors. It bolted, ripping the rope from John Joe's grip then slammed right into Billy's boxer sinking its teeth into the side of its neck. The boxer yelped as they rolled on top of each other. It wouldn't let go sinking its fangs in further going for the jugular and drawing blood. Billy still had his boxer on the lead and it was getting wrapped up around them both as the two dogs rolled all over the floor. Billy let go. Then the buzzer rang.

When Danny and Ana got outside the night shelter it was past closing. They stood shivering in the cold air waiting for the door to be answered but nobody came to the door. Danny tried again then Ana pressed the buzzer keeping her finger on it.

"Tyson, Tyson." John Joe kicked his dog hard in the backside. It still wouldn't let go. He kicked it harder, it let go for a second, twisted round growling at its owner then the boxer sunk its jaws into the pit-bull's rump. Soon they were latched onto one another again rolling around under the tables snarling growling and spittle blood spraying the floor. Both dogs were of equal size and equal measure pound for pound all muscle and teeth. All the time the front door buzzer kept ringing.

Eventually Mary answered the door, looked at them both and shouted for Kenny. Kenny came to the door he was manager but looked more like a rough sleeper himself. "You haven't registered Ana, you know the rules you're supposed to register."

"Register what is this?" said Ana."

"Your name in the book at the centre you know the rules."

"Please it's freezing everything wet warm inside."

"No, rules are rules" said Kenny.

"For fucks sake" shouted Danny. He never lost his rag. "Let her in what do you think this is a Christmas turkey?" he said pointing to Ana's bump.

"Maybe we could bend them just this once?" said Mary.

"No, rules are rules."

"Please why you not help me?" Ana tried to push past them both but Kenny forced the door shut. Ana put her finger on the buzzer again.

"Stand back get back no one get closer get back!" John Joe hollered the leads getting more tangled up in the dogs. Everybody moved back. Kenny was doing his best to calm the situation down, all the time the buzzer sounding. Finally the dogs let go of each other and the owners got back control of their animals and leads. After what seemed like an eternity Kenny went back to open the door. Danny stood with his arm around Ana trying to calm her down as she was crying and shaking with the cold.

"Please I stay here tonight you know me I good person sorry I no sign book."

"There's no room, you can't stay here, go back to camp." Ana grabbed Danny's arm.

"Please Danny say something." Kenny looked at Danny and shook his head. Ana grabbed Kenny's arm.

"Please let go of my arm," Kenny said calmly enough but she kept hold. Billy pushed by Kenny with a whimpering boxer beside him, opening the door wide in order to get past the group huddled at the door, as the door opened the icy blast hit them and ruffled everything inside.

"Room now Ana stay no go back camp too much dangerous too much heroin shit heads why you not help?"

Mary came back to the door. "I called the police, there's nothing we can do for you now go."

Ana tried to push past them both and they blocked her path pushing her away. Ana spat in their faces. Just then Danny heard a car pull up behind him he turned around and saw the police panda car. Two police officers got out zips done right up to their chins shivering. He looked back at Kenny and Mary, wiping the spit from their faces.

"Taxi for Ana," Danny said. No one laughed. The police stood there with their arms folded in front of their chests glaring at Ana.

"Ana are we going to do this the hard way or are you going to cooperate?"

"You arrest me." She was calm again.

"Do you want me to arrest you?" said the constable.

"I do," said Kenny.

"Okie dokie baby." She held out her wrists, "You cuff me."

"No need for that if you come quietly."

"Sorry very much Danny." She kissed Danny and gave him a long hug. "Don't worry you my friend forever love you very much."

"I know I love you very much."

"I know one hundred percent."

"Come on taxi's waiting." The female officer led Ana to the car and they waited in the back seat. Constable Smith waited outside.

"If you two go back in I will speak to you later I just need a quick word with Danny."

"Danny you ok mate you don't look good?"

"It's Ana I dunno what to do, she's gonna have the baby any second she ain't got anywhere to live. Can't you do something it's an emergency?" Danny felt himself welling up.

"She's not done herself any favours," said Smith. "They have offered her places but she's turned them down. They tried to help but they can't really do anymore. She wants to live here but there are no places here."

"Why not?"

"Look, they won't give her a place here. She can't look after herself. How's she going to take care of a baby?

The baby will be taken into care as soon as it's born, she must realise that. If it was that bad she would take anywhere, it's four walls, it shouldn't matter where it is."

"Yes but she's sick in the head. Can't you section her or something, find her a bed up the hospital?"

"The courts decided that she's capable of making her own decisions. It's not simple. She tries to manipulate the police the courts probation you. She tries to manipulate everyone. Their main priority is the baby. To be honest they don't really care much about her."

"She's not well," pleaded Danny.

"I know it's hard to accept it's cold but that's the way it is she won't get the help here she's not entitled the council are not legally obliged to provide her with a home." His radio came on, he answered. "Danny we have to go."

Danny noticed an AA poster pinned to the trunk of a tree. It showed a picture of a man curled up inside a bottle with iron bars like a prisoner. No doubt nailed to the tree with altruistic intentions by social reformers as a source of motivation and encouragement to the park's scallywags. Alas the message didn't have the power to penetrate their thick skulls.

All the arseholes had gathered together, telling lies and exaggerating about the amount of money they had begged, the whiskey they had drunk and the dope they had smoked. Building each other up on pedestals only to knock them down and stick in the knives and twist them in the next breath.

They all dressed for the race track but never broke a sweat except from chemical or alcoholic withdrawal. They couldn't run fifty yards without collapsing from a coronary. They were all manipulative and cunning, sometimes charming the birds from the trees but covertly hostile and domineering. Seeing other people merely as an instrument to be used and abused and disposed of like a piece of rubbish when they have no further use for them. Grandiose pathological liars who didn't see others around them as human beings but as targets and opportunities. Callous, lacking in empathy for their fellow man feeling only contempt for other people's feelings of distress and always ready to take advantage. Oblivious and indifferent to the devastation they cause. Putting it simply – scum. This park was their Mecca, the centre of their tiny universe. Their cardboard coliseum of pointless drama and violence. Danny watched them all watering the flower beds as the ground around them vibrated to an ethnic thumping beat.

Spencer hid in the bushes like a sniper with his forty million pickles, zooming in on the small group of dealers and drunks fooling about around the benches, screaming and jumping on each other's backs the other side of the park. A motley crew of physically damaged and mentally deranged individuals who urinated over the flower beds and grass. Some walking round in circles like zombies, others high on spice frozen like statues.

As this was all playing out Spencer was slowly making his way towards the group, occasionally dropping to one knee and firing off a few shots. Spencer zoomed in on a couple of girls coming out of the toilets. They looked attractive from a distance but zooming up closer in the cold light of day he saw one had a broken nose and a scar on her chin, and the other girl was just as hideous. They sat down on the bench next to the strangest of creatures, his face was covered in bumps and scratches, he was wearing a dress and high heels but there was something else. His arms and legs were covered in razor blade scars about an inch long, there must have been hundreds of them. Tiny inch long white scars glistening in the sun. He fired off a couple more shots.

Spencer smiled to himself. You could see all the gory details in glorious high resolution explicit in its detail, something he could really exploit. But the man was a damaged human being who had suffered in his life from the most horrendous forms of abuse you could imagine. Nobody liked him, they tolerated him, pitied him really. He stayed with the group for protection, sharing the money he got by selling himself to weirdos in the toilet for ten pounds a blow. A tragic case, a psychiatric nightmare.

The group hadn't taken much notice of Spencer up to now having left him relatively alone, but he was slowly edging precariously closer. Risking life and limb for the perfect shot he caught the attention of a member of the group, who gave him the V sign. Unperturbed he headed his way foolishly closer.

"Nice equipment," Ana said, the others sniggered maliciously. "Nikon?"

"Canon actually"

"Taken any good snaps?" Ana asked.

"Take a picture of this darling." A woman turned her back to him, pulled down her knickers and showed him the moon of her arse as the others cackled.

"Fucking cunt snapper," someone said.

"You want a close up?" Ana said. "How about this?" She raised her dress revealing her vagina and squealed.

"Do you mind if I take your photos? It's for a book I'm doing," he said like a Muppet.

"Cost you," said Ana.

"How much?"

"Fifty."

"How about twenty?"

"Done."

He began to fire off the shots in rapid succession like he was on location somewhere exotic. He beamed widely as women postured and blew kisses at him. After he had finished snapping Clara the tallest and better looking of the group sauntered provocatively towards him. Slowly she pressed her finger into the middle of his chest, slowly ran it down to his navel blew in his ear. Then in a slow and seductive voice she propositioned him.

"If you're interested?" she said. Spencer gulped. "Let's get away from these boring bastards I'd much rather spend time with you," she said.

Spencer showed his true colours. Stepping over an old drunk lying on the toilet steps she looked loaded as she led him through the toilets and into a small cramped room. Inside that dimly lit cell with her back towards him she dropped to her knees and hoisted up her dress to reveal her curvaceous thighs and shapely bottom. Spencer felt faint and leered hungrily as he fired off a few more shots, the flash illuminating the squalid room. He moved up close behind her and kissed her shoulders, arms then slowly worked his way down her spine. Spencer felt things stirring in his loins so he removed his trousers. Spencer sensed her sweet smelling body as he gently squeezed his manhood between her legs. It was tight his body spasmed and jerked as he pushed and coursed the ninety degree struggle. Rolling and writhing on top of her like two sweaty dogs, inside her cramped space, inside that cramped space in ecstasy slowly meeting a climax throbbing and pumping hard until he ejaculated.

She pulled out slowly and turned towards Spencer. Clara removed his curly wig from his head then threw away his dress from his body, baring his hairy chest and further down revealing his terrible secret. As he stood before Spencer with his big part swinging between his legs, Spencer shell shocked full of the fear of God gaped in sheer terror cold shivers raced down his spine, his whole body drained of life. Like a rabbit in the headlights he froze. Coming to his senses he scrambled about on the floor trying to gather up his clothes and expensive equipment. He was trapped and couldn't seem to find the door, running round the confined space like a frightened rat. Crashing out the door he ran screaming up the steps and hurtled arse over elbow outside, barefooted clutching hold of his shoes, trousers and precious Canon. Passers-by stopped in their tracks to see what was happening watching a half-naked man running across the park clutching his possessions for dear life.

Danny saw the rabble gathering around Clara; he saw Ana hiding obscured by the mob, she was making an exchange with Aaron. Then she disappeared.

"You again." Aaron gloated as Danny approached him.

"Where's Ana gone?"

"In't carzi fucking like a lurcher for fifty sobs."

"Ana?"

"Everyone's had that bitch," said a ginger ape standing in Aaron's shadow which sent sounds of craved laughter reverberating around. "Dirty whore."

"Lend me fifty sobs," said one of the mob shoving a Cornish pasty in his mouth like a pig.

"What you on about?" said Danny.

"Does she swallow or spit it out?" Food falling from his mouth he was looking for a reaction but Danny wasn't in the mood.

"Come on lad she never fucked with thee." Danny remained quiet.

"Not even sucked thy's tiny dick." The laughter died down. Aaron came right up to him invading his personal space he could smell his rank breath and said quietly. "Seriously didn't thee know she was a whore? Last night I was so far up her I…"

A great rush of rage slammed through Danny like rocket fuel. Danny went for him but before he could land the punch he was dropped like a sack of potatoes. Aaron looked down at him. "Ye gods thee really are a crazy bastard." Danny lay on the muddy earth groaning. "Shut up woman." They walked off.

After searching around the park for what seemed like hours Danny eventually found Ana. There was a strange solitude and silence that possessed that quiet secluded corner. High up the setting sun cast its final rays over them, as she stood in front of him shrouded in an incredible white light. She took a drag and seemed in a very relaxed state. She pulled at her hair band, tossed back her hair, kicked off her shoes and groaned pleasantly. Pacing around barefoot in the shallow puddles kicking up water from the surface, rolling her head around and screeching with delight. Clapping her hands above her head as if trying to catch imaginary flying insects, kicking up water waving her arms. Swatting at the hallucinogenic butterflies. Screeching walking in circles. It confused Danny, it bewildered him, terrified him inside as she walked around the corner of the park. Danny sat on the edge of the fountain watching her. A chaotic mass of morbid unwanted thoughts raced round his head like spaghetti junction exhausting him to the brink. She was uneasy on her feet taking a drag laughing and stumbling, her voice slurring and rambling along.

There was a beautiful golden sun on the horizon just about to set but his heart sank upon the sight of her in the distance, as she suddenly collapsed. Danny ran over, dropped to his knees beside her.

Ana clutched her stomach and groaned, "Pain help me."

"Is it the baby?"

"No, I don't know."

Dazed and confused she muttered in a weak voice as she gazed upon him in a trance. She began to bang her head against the grass making facial contortions and foaming at the mouth. Her body, hands and head all together in a ceaseless flailing frenzy. Danny sat there helpless and panic stricken.

"Help," she managed to mumble as she twisted her head around, body shaking and thrashing on the earth. She tried to lift herself but she couldn't. Then she went limp and lifeless Danny held her hand tight, her nails digging into his palm then her body went weak and her hand fell from his grasp. He stroked her hair and shook her gently; her eyes flickered as he held her in his arms.

The paramedics came first and started working on her checking for a pulse and airwaves for vital signs of life. Questions, insinuations, accusations. "What's she taken?" Danny covered his face with his hands. They started breathing into her mouth and thumping her chest, then they charged up the portable defibrillator. Jolts of electricity charged through her lifeless body. Danny felt the pain he felt it charge out but he was staring death in the face. She coughed, her eyes flickered and opened wide as saucers hair flapping in the wind.
"Novak," she said.
Nausea crept against Danny's lungs as he sat speechless in the blue flickering electric light.
"One two three lift," from the grass to the stretcher and into the ambulance. She blacked out.
She woke and opened her eyes, the room came into focus. Every ounce of her flesh dull with pain a mechanical irregular beeping noise. Every breath she takes hurts. Muffled voices muffled footsteps muffled rumbling of trolley wheels outside the door. Her left arm covered in a thick pad of gauze, plastic tube inserted into her arm, connected to a clear bottle of fluid, strapped to a metal pole, a nurse stood over her.
Ana shifted around in her bed and tried pulling the saline drip from her arm. "No," the nurse shouted, trying to restrain her, holding her arms away. Ana lashed out and tried to get out of bed but she couldn't.

"Wait here," said the nurse.

The student nurse left the room and hot footed it down the corridor to the nursing station. Doctors and nurses were all flying around in starched white coats and blue uniforms, rushing in and out of cubicles, carrying bandages, clip boards and bits of foam. In the corridor a woman on a pair of crutches crashed backwards to the floor. She looked at the nurse as she came hurtling towards her and came skidding to a halt. She glared at the nurse as if she might die. A doctor started yelling at her to get some insulin as the woman started shaking violently on the floor and a colleague put a blanket over her shaking limbs. Outside the nursing station a man was screaming his lungs out.

Entering the nursing station she explained about Ana, collected the insulin and the two nurses ran back up the blue line, past the ranting man to the woman fitting on the floor. She gave the insulin to the doctor and ran back to Ana with help.

"No Ana put back the drip." Both nurses grappled with her and managed to put the drip back in her arm. Ana went calm for a few moments, the nurse sat down on her bed exasperated. Ana started pulling at the drip again, the student nurse ran back down the corridor, a couple of paramedics crashed through a side door almost colliding with her pushing a man in a wheelchair who was coughing up blood into a plastic bowl. They bolted past her and smashed through a set of double doors. Outside the nursing station the man was still ranting in the grip of a psychotic episode.

Lying on the corridor floor the woman was still in the throes of an epileptic seizure. Overwhelming chaos the nurse just days on the job didn't know where she was, she stopped to help. Lifting the woman from the floor to a trolley the doctor shone a bright light in the patient's eyes, she lurched and vomited all over the nurse. Two porters took over and the nurse rushed away.

Ana struggled with the nurses and she pulled the drip from her arm, blood trickled down her wrist and she held it up laughing as blood drained from the nurse's face. Ana started screaming and the nurse cracked from the pressure and started to cry.

"I want to go I not stay here," Ana screamed. The doctor turned to the young nurse and asked her to leave, she pressed the panic button. Two security piled in and pulled the curtain around the bed. All you could hear was a barrage of abuse, then silence. Ten seconds later they come out. "Sorry we had to sedate her." They looked red faced and wrapped with exhaustion.

"Clean yourself up immediately, you're covered in vomit, it's unhygienic," he told the nurse.

"I know I'm sorry," she said, just holding it together.

~ ~ ~

Ana could sense her brother's ghost on the peripheral of her senses, he bore her no malice. She was getting used to him, growing indifferent to his presence seeking comfort trapped between the physical and spiritual realms.

The vodka from last night had crystallised inside her, she put the water bottle to her lips and drank. Melting the sediment alcohol evaporated into her bloodstream and began to flow around her.

The rising sun filtering through the window broke her physical and spiritual darkness, soaking the curtains around her bed in a fiery hue as she lay in alcoholic melancholic saturation. Swamped by the elements her past tangibly manifest played out on the screen around her.

Approaching her village the landscape began to change. The tall evergreens now ever charred black the leaves scorched, they loomed like the skeletons around her. At the fork road there lay no fork, just rubble, the roundabout a deep pool of ash emanating a corrosive smell.

The black walls of the houses exposed the furniture inside like a burnt dolls house. The abandoned vehicles covered in a thick white carpet of dust. Alarms blazed out all over the village and deserted streets. Precious memories of a lifetime destroyed in a few minutes. Lives shattered bodies buried beneath the burning embers. Burnt out tanks and cars on the highway, broken men and women carrying everything they had left on their backs heading for the border.

~ ~ ~

Danny could see her through the glass window of the special baby unit, sitting with her back to him next to the cot. After he removed his coat and disinfected his hands he went in. He looked in the cot but he couldn't see anything. Then he glanced at Ana and she had the tiniest bundle in her arms, just a few hours old.

"Hello Danny. This is my son." Niagara falls. Danny couldn't control his emotions and broke down completely.

"No cry you man not baby." Ana's social worker was standing next to them looking at all the other babies in the unit which were considered special measures or at risk. Danny kissed Ana on the head. It was a relief and a miracle the baby was in good health.

"Ana we have to talk," said the social worker.

"Danny come to?" She looked him up and down then nodded. They wheeled Ana into a small room, Danny was still sobbing. Rachel the social worker and Maria the interpreter sat in front of them. Rachel started to speak to Ana about how she was feeling about the future of her children and what they had discussed in previous sessions. The interpreter spoke when it got more complicated. Sometimes it felt like an interrogation but Ana remained calm, but the conversation got more heated.

"Ana you have had three abortions in three years." Danny didn't know, he looked shocked. "Two up to the maximum legal term, haven't you heard of contraception?"

"No me no contraception me Catholic no contraception," she lied.

"I didn't think the Catholic Church believed in abortions either." Ana was silent. "You have repeatedly turned down all our offers of help, your sister told us you haven't spoken to your daughter in two years." So Ana had a daughter, that was another shock for Danny to take in.

"Lies, lies," said Ana.

"Do you have trouble bonding with your children?"

"I love my children please just quickly job home my children can stay with me here England."

"Why haven't you spoken to her in two years?"

"I get job in factory I get contract."

"Your sister thinks you're an unfit mother."

"Bullshit my sister never says this."

"What's more important Ana, drink, drugs or your children?"

"I stop drink drugs I promise no more finish I spend money on baby Jesus now." There was an elephant in the room impossible to ignore.

"You have no money, how?"

"I don't know I get job quickly I change please no take my son. You no take my son. I his mother, he my son, no, I stop everything now I stop I promise."

"You have to prove to us you can stop."

"I have nothing, why you hate me, you no my friend, why you all hate me?"

"We offered you a place in a special mother and baby unit in London, with round the clock help and support, we offered you accommodation in various places. We tried to help but you have repeatedly turned down all our efforts. You refused to talk to us when we came to the centre looking for you, you hardly attend meetings."

"He's not your son he's my son."

"Do you know who the father is?"

"His father not important."

"You don't know who the father is, how many sexual partners have you had in the last year?"

"I pregnant."

"You're always. I have a report from probation you have been arrested six times this year for public order offences. Drunk and disorderly, affray, criminal damage, assault, assault on a police officer, you said in court I quote. 'I like fight I like drink I like cause trouble'. Do you think you have a drug and alcohol problem? How much marijuana do you smoke?"

"Just little."

"We will conduct tests. You will be tested monthly for use of all illegal substances from now on. You will be given three months to find yourself suitable accommodation and suitable employment. You must remain clean for three months then we will review your situation. You must not get into any more trouble with the police or you will be deported back to Bosnia and you will lose everything. We will no longer try to help you. Your son is to be made a ward of court, this child is not to leave the hospital. You are free to visit anytime but if you attempt to remove him anytime you will be arrested. You will appear in court in a month to discuss foster care and visiting privileges. You must attend this hearing or you will jeopardise your chances of ever getting your son back. Do you understand?"

"Yes."

"Do you agree to the terms and conditions?"

"Yes."

Danny said goodbye to Ana and left. He was knackered and his mind was all over the place. He spent half an hour trying to find the exit. He followed the red line until it turned green, but landed in Orthopaedics. Yellow lines, blue lines, green lines and red lines merging. Orthopaedic, Geriatric, Cardiology and Urology passing doctors, nurses and porters and cleaners back to maternity again before he escaped.

~ ~ ~

The unmistakable sound of a hurricane engine could be heard. It carried on the wind and soon it burst through the hazy clouds to reveal itself. The sun gleaming on its fuselage, soaring higher and higher into the deep blue yonder, its engines whirled. Obscured by the sun it dipped its wing and peeled to the left. Swooping low coasting through the clouds it plummeted to earth. It lifted from its dive just yards from the sea, and completed the manoeuvre. It climbed higher and higher in a giant curve then up again with increasing speed in a mighty arc. It rose above the clouds looping the loop. Shielding his eyes from the sun, Danny watched it advancing.

Looking back down from where he stood leaning against the wall of the Methodist church he saw Ana approaching him from across the street. She was clean, well dressed, had a healthy glow and her eyes were bright. Her eyes were full of the fear of God.

She saw the aircraft screaming over the water, spitting a hail storm of lead from its guns. Spluttering a staccato of bullets over the choppy sea. Advancing shoreward ripping up the beach scattering the crowd blinded by the stinging spray of pebble and sand.

She fell to her knees. She looked up through the clearing cloud of acrid smoke. A miasma of rotting flesh drifted towards her on the tide. Fragments of flesh, bone and hair blasted across a hundred yard stretch. Disembodied, disembowelled, decapitated corpses littered the earth and hung from barbed wire fences dripping blood to the sand. Danny stood over her.

Ana had a place in a halfway house and a job. It was part time but it was a start.

"Go inside, have some tea, it's freezing out here," she said.

"Yes," Danny agreed.

The church was surrounded by a brick wall with a cast iron gate, which enclosed a small garden. Two benches sat under the bows of some apple trees, which bore fruit in summer but were now in their spring dress of white and pink blossom. On the door hung the familiar AA and NA blue sign.

They walked along the path of wind-blown white and pink blossoms and went inside. The warmth hit them in more ways than one. The room had a high ceiling with a piano in the corner. There was a table with two chairs at one end and about thirty chairs arranged in a semi-circular pattern in front. A table at the back had an arrangement of books and pamphlets and there were two large banners hanging from the walls displaying the twelve steps and twelve traditions.

Danny went up to the tea counter with Ana but his hands were shaking. A woman was behind the counter serving tea. "Hi guys!" she said. "Tea?"

"I'm a bit shaky," Danny said.

"Okay I'll give you half a cup."

Danny and Ana sat down next to the piano, Danny's hands still shaking so he sat down on them. Ana told Danny all about the halfway house. She was forty next week but she felt like she had been given a second chance in life. She felt like she had just stepped out of a dark cave and into the sunlight. She said that for the first time in a long time she felt hope. Everyone looked happy and well, everyone was a miracle of recovery. Everyone had been in the same boat and escaped disaster together. They knew each other's bones and the calcium and blood that swam within.

Ana lifted the lid and started to play the piano. Trying to remember the notes she slowly got control of the rhythm. Danny didn't recognise the tune but it was classical, it was beautiful, such sensitivity he had a lump in his throat. Everyone stopped talking, everyone started to listen, no one breathed, such spellbinding melancholia.

She stopped. "I no remember the name this song I play for Pope in Vatican I forget what is called maybe Mozart, Schubert not Chopin." Danny welled up she was still so sick but getting better. "No drink no drug three months one day at a time."

After the hubbub had died down and everyone had taken a seat George welcomed everyone to the meeting. After the preambles he introduced the afternoon's guest speaker. It was a tale of near fatal overdoses and everything life could dump on you.

When the meeting was over they went outside and Ana showed Danny endless photographs of the baby on her phone.

"How is he?" Danny asked.

"Beautiful, no one takes my son no one."

"No."

"I was bad mother."

"Yes you were but you can change, we can both change. I won't lie to you, I will never lie to you. I'm your friend. A real friend speaks the truth. I hate what we became. I hate what the drugs, the drink had done to us. But that's not the real us. The real us, the good us, is still inside, it will be hard to get back, but we can do it together. We can change if we really want to." They headed off in the direction of the underpass.

"No deportation no way."

"We're sick, we need help. I don't think we should stay here. I think it will be too difficult to get better. We should go somewhere else and start again."

On entering the subway they ran into Magda. Magda was a young Croatian girl from the outreach team. She was busy with her friends handing out food parcels and pouring out hot tea from her Thermos flask. She did this every day. They said hello, Ana started talking to Magda in Croatian then she went over to the other side of the tunnel to a man who slept under a white duvet cover and she gave him some sandwiches. When Ana saw them she went ballistic.

Ana started shouting and screaming at Magda in her native tongue. Magda just stood there and took it, Danny grabbed Ana by the shoulders and told her to calm down.

"No! No give this man food this man sex with children this man monster!" Danny couldn't really tell what was going on. "I know what you did you not wanted here go leave I kill you I swear!"

"Okay this is the case but he is still a person who is hungry he needs food," replied Magda.

"I don't believe this you know what this is Magda, you have brother ten years you like this man have sex with him?" she shouted.

Magda looked shocked they stood staring each other out like a couple of gunfighters in the old West. Ana drew first. "Why this man not prison why this man not dead you give me gun I kill him I promise." The man stayed hidden under the duvet. "I kill you Russian Mafia." She pretended to shoot him. Danny looked around nervously hesitantly he moved forwards. The head popped out from underneath the duvet. Danny felt his heart explode in his chest and dropped to his knees with shock.

No qualms about it, the world would be a better place without him. Danny had contemplated the idea for an eternity. It had ceased to have any emotional attachment, the death of him.

Released on bail? If the courts didn't care he would have to do something about it himself. Exact his own justice. The poisonous lichen of hatred spread in his heart. Danny sank deeper into the indent of his mattress. Deeper into the quagmire of his despair.

His hatred for him fed and glutted itself on the thought of his ruin. His hatred festered inside and glutted and fed on his own ruin. He had allowed himself to be shackled and chained. Second by second minute on minute hour after hour week over week year after bloody year of his life.

His noose grew tighter and tighter around his neck as he choked and struggled to no avail, his abuser slept oblivious to his torture. Danny dwelt on that thought for a moment. Justice was slow so he would have to provide a swifter justice for the long strangulation he had suffered.

He remembered how the first notion of killing him had manifested a mustard seed that he had tossed into the long barren grass. A germ of an idea in his fertile imagination which sprouted fragile tendrils in the dark earth took root and began to grow in the sun and rain. Over time it took bud and sprouted leaves. All through his life it had flourished and grown into a tree fed on hate. Hooded crows came to nest and cry as he walked under its shadow and listened.

This disease, this malaise, this thorny bush of thought was not confined to the dirty city streets. It spread through the air on poisonous spores that infected the air. Hopped like the bed bugs mattress to mattress multiplying and feeding off its host growing fat.

His obsession was his constant companion. Danny flicked his lighter and all around him were shadows of men. The lumpy mattress they gave him at the shelter was an ecstasy of relief compared to the cold hard pavements. The only dilemma was how to open a can quietly enough to avoid being set upon. Under the cover of blankets under the cover of darkness he muffled the sound.

He put the drink to his lips and its warmth bloomed inside him, took away the fear. Soon the ocean swell of exhaustion pulled him under and he succumbed to sleep.

~ ~ ~

Ana thought she could hear something scratching behind the cellar door, so she knelt down on the cold concrete wincing as a sharp piece of glass or brick dug into her kneecaps. Moving position she looked through the keyhole, but all she could see was thick darkness and indiscriminate shapes and edges jutting out the gloom. Ear to the door she heard a faint rustling sound, which she decided must have been a rat. She hated rats as much as she hated that sick bastard Peter the paedophile and classed them both as vermin.

She sniffed the air at the keyhole, and an acrid smell emanated from within the gloom of misshapen old boxes of old clothes, empty bottles magazines and miscellaneous drugs paraphernalia. Which the old bastard who lived there had built up over the years and hoarded and squirreled away in every conceivable nook and cranny of the squat as well as the wall cavities. A reflection of the state of his own sick and twisted mind.

People had told her that the old man was friends with Peter, and Peter was sleeping down there in the cellar. There is only one way to flush out a rat, she thought.

She poured some paraffin through the keyhole, lit a match and dropped it in. A flash of orange lit up the space between the bottom of the door frame and the floor. Thick black smoke started pouring through the keyhole and seeped under the door. Smoke started curling up to the ceiling and spread down the corridor as the flames began to lick the inside of the door, and billowed black smoke into the basement. The air in the cellar was thick in seconds, the old tramp started coughing violently as he put his scarf against his face and coughed black mucus into it.

The smoke was so heavy now he could hardly see. He managed to climb the stairs felt for the key in the lock, burning his hand he dropped the key. He tried pushing the door but it wouldn't open. The flames licked his trousers so he ran down stairs. The basement windows which just poked above street level were barred by thick iron crosses too small to climb through. By the grace of God in the corner of the basement was an axe. The tramp ran up the stairs and lunged at the wooden door splintering it. The sudden gush of air filled the vacuum with oxygen and the fire ripped.

The inferno took hold gathering at the top of the stairs and in a rolling crackling carpet of flames it started to descend the staircase. Half way down it ignited a case of vodka that exploded into red and purple flames and came crashing and burning down, slamming against the cellar wall. Bouncing onto the floor the carpet of flames grew in intensity and started to lick the corner of his tent. The flames climbed slowly melting the plastic turning it from blue to black as it slowly disintegrated. The air in the room boiled as the ice in the innocent victims veins froze.

The windows blew out shattering the heavy panes fanning the inferno and jagged splinters of glass rained down. The fire breathed in the oxygen in greedy gulps and roared. The floor, walls and ceilings engulfed the cellar, more bottles of vodka exploded like bombs. The walls channelling the flames like a chimney bought the staircase down and the old tramp was buried under the rubble of wood coughing and wheezing in the black pungent air. His eyes and lungs burned, his hands grasped at nothing as he was consumed in the fireball.

PART FOUR

The gusting wind began to die away into a strange silence. The rising sun fell upon her and the shadows of passing clouds glided over like spirits as the sunbeams watery rays lit up her solitude.

Her eyes dark as the night, contrasted with her olive skin, burnt with intensity. Danny was afraid to know all that possessed the depths of that girl's lonely spirit.

A cut was sunk deep in her forehead, track marks ran down her arms. She raised her languid head then lowered it to the ground then raised up her arms to her God once again, as she fervently prayed. Praying from the depths of her soul, her praying was fevered but frantic in despair.

Her body heaved unhindered in rhythm, occasionally grabbing her hair as if to tear it to shreds, her fingers entwined among the tresses. Her mouth moved incessantly, in a deep modulated voice she began to wail rhythmical verse that slowly rolled through the air, filling the void with powerful vibrations.

Her stream of words poured into him unopposed, veraciously he absorbed their radiations which overwhelmed the equilibrium in its swelling tones. For several minutes she continued with her flagellations until the volume overwhelmed the secluded alleyway, making itself palpable to the senses. The moment of dissolution was at hand.

In an instant all was still. The grabbing of her locks, the heaving, breathing and wailing ceased. Her lips were open but the breath of fervour that had ebbed and flowed between them had completed and damp distillation soaked her brow. The force of prayer left her body exhausted, spent and shrunken up within, collapsed upon her mat.

Ana raised her head from her droop and gazed vacantly out of her hypnotic eyes at Danny. Fixing him in a phantom like glare he looked into her shattered face.

Restlessness and discontentment had become a chronic manifestation. Like a ship adrift from its moorings her broken chains and anchor trailed noisily after her rocking ominously and unsteadily adrift on the ocean waves and landed on a different lonely shore.

Demure in her black robes that flapped in the wind and wrapped the contours of her figure, Danny's soul seemed to melt in her hypnotic gaze. Casting his eyes down at her sandaled feet and slowly examining the rest of her body, she oozed sex. She spoke in a fast and excitable manner, her accent a strange mix of English and Balkan which alternated constantly. Her black braids looked like a basket of wriggling grass snakes on her head. Falling across her eyes she shook and jerked, in conjunction with her penetrating eyes she had the look of a medusa.

"Danny I sense you afflicted with a most terrible burden you should come pray with me. It is said that upon the presence of Allah men and women have thrown away their sticks and walked again."

"I don't believe in any Gods."

"Don't speak such nonsense my child, for Allah will see fit in his powers unknown to you to help you walk again."

"What powers?"

"Infinite divine powers, you shall bear witness to his healing, we must go now." She pulled his arms and the robes clung to her flesh. Danny resisted. He looked up into the boiling cauldron of clouds.

"Looks like rain."

"Always rain this country."

He wasn't sure that it was wise but somehow he felt obligated to follow.

She guided him through the back alleyways of the city, marching along with others like an advancing army towards the temple. They followed the crowd of poor deluded people in Danny's opinion. He believed all their minds had been twisted and fed into believing their souls would be saved and blessed, the sick and lame be healed. But Allah was no more real or sacred to him than any other Gods. No more real or sacred than the plastic effigies or glow in the dark symbols that hung around their necks. There were young and old, rich and poor, black and white, some on crutches, many in wheelchairs, some walking with cuts and blisters on their bare feet.

There were small signs with arrows tied to drain pipes. They followed the signs and arrows before arriving at the destination. The crumbling Victorian brick façade resembled an old warehouse. A group of men were hanging around outside, they brushed past them and went inside. Inside the door was a table overladen with copies of the Quran, on the floor a huge pile of shoes. Ana kicked off her sandals and grabbed Danny by the arm.

"Please remove your shoes." As Danny concurred an odour pervaded the lobby. An old lecherous man had his eyes fixed on Ana like glue, looking her up and down, she noticed and felt troubled.

Inside the imposing room he felt the four walls closing in on him. On the wall in front of him was a large blow up picture of Mecca laid on the floor in front of a long line of prayer mats. Danny looked around nervously; he felt strangely disconnected from his unexpected situation and felt trapped. Just to the side was a large portrait of the prophet Mohammad, the sun behind his head with rays emanating glaring down upon him.

When the service had ended a bewildered and discombobulated Danny looked around the mosque to see if he could see Ana. But she was obscured by so many people and had just melted into the background of black robes, hijabs and burkas. Two very heavy set men uneasy on their feet staggered through the congregation. A woman that may or may not have been Ana came walking towards them dressed in black. She tried to walk past but they deliberately blocked her path. Then they made a grab for her and pushed her against the wall.

Danny ran forwards but two men grabbed him and hurriedly pulled him away. Danny heard Ana screaming. He turned fast to see that they were dragging her away. She was kicking and lashing out at them. Danny tried to break free from the two men but they held him back, and he watched helplessly as she was carried out the building.

~ ~ ~

The following day Danny was back on the street desperately searching for Ana when he heard the familiar sound of an acoustic guitar being played, he half recognised the tune. As he got closer he saw a man, his guitar case on the ground half full of coppers and penny chews. Danny dropped a few coins inside.

"Many thanks, my friend," he said. Danny stood next to him and listened a while until he stopped. "What I really need is a proper band, you know, the whole ensemble. It sounds much better with bells and whistles, you can't really do it justice with just a guitar," he continued.

"Have they found Ana?" he asked him. A look of dread came over his face.

"Look my friend, I've heard bad things about those men, really bad things."

"Like what?"

"They sell more drugs than Pfizer, and I have heard from several people that they like to drug up young girls and have their evil way with them, sometimes they pimp them, out get their friends round to sample the goods, they're evil my good friend."

"Do you know where I can find them?"

"No."

Danny set out to try and find her. The city felt more intimidating at night, filling up with drunk students and idiots who were out looking for trouble. They wouldn't have a good night until they found it. They were walking around like they meant business. While a panda car slowly cruised the high street keeping a lookout, thumping music was blasting through the night sky. There was a group of people outside the library talking, smoking, drinking cans of beer and generally fooling around to heavy thumping bhangra beat. Danny recognised someone from the church in a pair of trousers shirtless and shivering. Danny felt too warm he had three jumpers on, so he took one of his off and gave it to him.

"You can borrow this, but I want it back." He took it, the others were too wrapped up in their smoking, drinking and dancing to take any notice.

"Do you know where Ana's has been taken?" Danny asked

"Those men?"

"Yes."

"They used to be friends of mine, till they sleep with my little sister and give her drugs."

"Where do they take them?"

He just shrugged. Danny continued through the city streets passed Frank sitting in Burger King's door way shouting at himself as he gulped down vodka. He was a big man, he looked like a monster, but he wasn't one. The left hand side of his face had dropped due to a bad operation, so his eyes didn't level up. Well there was just a hole for his right eye all closed up. He had a big dent on his forehead in the shape of a household iron and a circular scar on his cheek. He sat outside the entrance of the takeaway in a bright orange high viz jacket with his rucksack spilt out all over the ground and a bottle of cider beside him. His first name was Amir but every one called him Frank – short for Frankenstein. He was sitting next to Suzi, she was not a dwarf but not far from it. They were a couple. She was the complete opposite to Frank who was well over six foot four even with his hunched shoulders. Her head barely reached above his waist. Suzi liked to set fire to people's tents after she had stolen items from inside them. They didn't know where Ana was.

Danny saw Billy and Brendan standing outside the Post Office. Brendan sang and Billy banged a tray over his head keeping time as he sang and slammed the tray. Danny didn't think Brendan possessed the most dulcet tones, it was more like a nasally whine. Musically he had an unusual delivery and at times he sounded like a dalek. Billy would bang the tray over his head until he had a migraine but it worked. Soon they had a whole crowd of people around them and throwing money. He thrashed out the tune upon his head and on the heads of passing drunks some of whom danced a jig for the growing audience. They were a big hit. Billy's head was swelling and bruised.

Danny didn't have time to hang around and watch. There was a woman standing on the street corner stopping people as they passed her and asking questions. She was holding a piece of paper in her hand. It looked like a map or perhaps a picture of some kind. As Danny got closer she stopped him and showed him a picture.

"Excuse me, have you seen this person?" she asked him then showed him the picture. The person in the photograph was unmistakable and his name was written in large letters underneath, 'Robbie'.

"Have you tried the park or the police station? He calls himself Jonah now, what's he done?" Danny looked at her scrutinizing her face. "I hope you don't mind me asking but who are you?"

"I'm his daughter," she replied. It was a shock to hear that. Danny often forgot that most of the rough sleepers have or have had families in their previous lives. But he didn't have time to chat.

"Sorry I have to go, maybe try the…"

"My mother is sick," she cut him short. "I don't think she's got long to go please I have to find him," she pleaded.

This put Danny in somewhat of a dilemma, but he had to help, and he knew where he was likely to be.

It didn't take long to find him. The best way to describe his doorway was between a shrine and Santa's grotto. He was another collector of junk who pushed around all his belongings in an old shopping trolley. He wore brightly coloured long flowing robes with bells and ribbons sewn on. He had long hair and a beard and looked like a wizard. Robbie used to have a flat but he accidentally burned it down. Most of the time he was confused, zoned out of his mind on weed and playing the kazoo or ranting like a maniac. He was ranting like a maniac when they found him.

He stopped dead when he saw his daughter but Danny left them to reacquaint themselves.

"Hey buddy!" It was Abdul sitting in a shop doorway wrapped up in a green sleeping bag. "How you doing?" he asked.

"Fine," replied Danny.

"Oh, so fucked-up, insecure, neurotic and emotional."

"That's about right." Danny sat down next to him and buried his head in his hands. Danny was cold now, he wished he hadn't given his spare jumper away. Abdul reached into his battered canvas bag, took out a heavy looking jacket then tossed it over to Danny. "Keep it."

Abdul was as pale as a ghost. He was gaunt looking with sunken cheeks and a large nose which made him look like a starving sparrow. He hadn't cut his hair in months, he had let himself go and that was an understatement, but his dog was in excellent health. People petted the dog and pitied him. Abdul's legs were so thin he hardly had the strength to stand up. His hands were red bloated and covered in calluses. He used to be a mod judging by his green bomber jacket, which was covered in old badges from various rallies, but they were old now and fading away to nothing. Just like himself.

"I'm looking for Ana, probably with some bloke called Omar she might be in danger."

"Shaggy Omar. The cherry picker?"

"Right you know where she might be?"

"Oh yeah."

After walking half a mile Danny turned left, passed Domino's pizza and through a narrow alley into a large housing estate. The windows shone like ribbons of golden light in the darkness. He saw a group of lads approaching him. There was probably no need to worry, just relax, he told himself. There were a few little street gangs in the city that liked to cause trouble. They were kids really that liked to swan around looking intimidating. They dressed in black and hung around in large groups in the parks and the edges of the estates. They would wheelie up and down on their mountain bikes, pick fights with foreigners, steal from shops and commit petty crime in an attempt to gain individual notoriety among their peers. Occasionally people would get hurt. They thought they were tough but in reality they were stupid little kids that needed to grow up.

Danny saw a girl, he didn't know if she was drunk or drugged up, a young lad was trying to carry her along the path, followed by four youths on their bikes all dressed in black with scarves wrapped around their faces. She was vulnerable without a doubt.

"You need any help mate?" Danny asked.

"No it's ok bruv don't need no help," one replied as they passed. At least he asked, Danny told himself.

"Get her to a hospital, bruv. I don't think the taxis will take her," he heard another say. They headed down a slope in the direction of the park. The young lad was struggling a bit with her, but he seemed genuinely concerned for her wellbeing. Danny watched them taking her down towards the park. She stood up but she was very wobbly, then she fell over and they crowded around her. Danny stayed put for a while and waited quietly watching the group in the park. He couldn't see what was going on with the girl because she was obscured by the group on bikes. Then he saw the park security approach in their high viz coats gleaming in the dark, so he continued.

Danny ran up the stairs to flat five and kicked open the door. He saw a man and a girl wrapped up in one another. Danny lifted the man off her and threw him off the bed.

"Scum," Danny yelled, "you arse hole you bastard."

"Relax have some weed bruv."

"Fucking rapist bastard"

"No."

"Yeah."

The man crawled over to the armchair and slumped down; he didn't seem in the least concerned. Danny was leaning over the girl shaking her trying to wake her up but she was out of it whoever she was.

"What did you give her?"
"I can't remember."
"I want to know."
"I can't tell you."
"Won't or can't, come on just tell me."
"I don't know."

Danny looked around the room and it was a mess. There were packets of weed wraps and all kinds of bottles with pills inside. He saw a rucksack on the floor, he slung it across the room, its contents flew out over the floor.

"You're a sick man," Danny said.
"It's only natural."
"She's twelve if she's a day."
"Makes it better."
"You're scum." Danny saw an empty bottle of vodka on the floor, grabbed it and smashed it against the wall. Its shattered glass flew everywhere, he held it against the man's throat, he let out a shriek of fear.

"Wa-wa-wait," he stammered." Let go please don't." Panic stricken he gulped for air greedily. "You're f-fucking mad."

"Probably but you're still scum."

"She wanted it she consented she was a willing partner."

Danny dropped the bottle, picked him up off the chair and pulled him over to her. "Look at her, look what you've done she wouldn't do it willingly so you had to drug her first. Do you know how they treat child rapists in prison? You could do twelve years."

"On what evidence? She won't go to the cops."
"No, but I will."

Danny threw the man's naked body against the wall where he smashed his head and remained on the floor half conscious. The girl was dead to the world moaning on the bed. Danny covered her over with the duvet. Danny removed the cable ties from his pockets, knelt down on the man's back and bound his hands and feet together. He sat down on the armchair and called the police.

~ ~ ~

The mist came creeping over the sea obscuring everything except the white caps of the waves through which the muttering of wind as if in deep distress drifted. The salt wind whirled the foam across the pebbles, distant voices muffled by the breeze heard between its soughs and moans. A deep and multitudinous voice far out to sea hushed a prelude to the symphony of the storm.

It starts at measured intervals only to be smothered by the shrill screams of sea birds. As the wind increased the birds sang more and grew thicker and thicker in the air above his head until there were hundreds gathered in the sky. All along the far running beach a rising tide of thick foam slithered across the pebbles. A gauze of light vapour clung upon the surface of the sea like rolling dew forwards and shorewards as the rising sun tried to burn through but was swallowed by the mist. The two flowed into each other but the light was sucked from the angry sea and sky and darkness fell like a guillotine.

It wallowed in the sea a shapeless mass rising and falling gently on the swell. Clouds of sea fowl whirled and hovered above, their wings smote pink by the rising sun. He saw it unravelling before him disappearing and re-emerging encroaching the shore.

Belched from the waves through the roar of the surface she rolled in on the brackish waters breaking over the sunken rocks. Swept by the winds dragnet her body floated through the soft butterscotch foam of the breaking waves. Landing on the loneliness of the sand split then rolling along the glistening surface of the pebbles under the thunder of the breakers that were chased up the beach by the roaring gale.

Danny ran up the beach towards her. Her nose and throat was full with sand, strangulated and wrapped in copious olive ribbons of glutinous seaweed. Her limbs a geography of blue and black marks, broken jaw, her tongue and lips had turned blue, head swollen up like a balloon, foam oozed from her twisted mouth, eyes pecked out by sea creatures. Sand hoppers danced on her flesh. He didn't recognise her.

Crunching shingle under foot for a hundred yards or so slanting himself into the gale Danny climbed through the barrier wind blasted with fragments of seaweed and sand which dug into his wet palms and stepped onto the promenade.

Weaving a path over fractured paving slabs, dog mess and smashed glass bottles in the gutter speckled with blood and diluted by the rain flowed down the drain. Nauseous with dread he walked past sinister dark gulls perched on the railings and felt they could read his mind.

Danny took sanctuary in a bus shelter as the rain poured profusely down. Through the haze he saw a lone figure come shambling towards him grinning and wheezing. Wrinkled skin stretched over bones, he gaped and moaned from his toothless jaws set in his bloated red face that hung on one side from his withered neck. Eyes bulging he slammed his fist against the plastic of the bus shelter which buffeted, creaked and groaned in the tempest of the storm as he cursed and demanded money to slake his thirst.

A crumpled half drunk can of beer and a soggy polystyrene box of a half eaten fish and chips supper lay discarded on the plastic seat. Danny gave it to him which he grabbed with his shrivelled hands like birds claws before he limped away.

~ ~ ~

"But why can't you just arrest them if you know who they are?"

"I wish it was that simple."

"Why not?"

"It's not like an episode of 'The Bill'. You can't wrap up an investigation in half an hour and bang up all the baddies. It takes time and money, you have to carry out proper investigations. You need money resources manpower."

"I don't understand."

"We are watching Omar and his crew but we need more evidence. Cast iron guarantees they won't get off on a technicality. We need proof, witness statements, lots of them. It's hard. Do you really think any of his girls are going to testify in court? That girl tried, we had to fish her out of the sea. I want to put them all away for a long time and throw away the key. They will get raided, they will go to prison eventually I promise you."

"Why can't you just arrest them with what you have now?"

"You haven't been listening have you? I told you for a start you need powers of search and arrest for a warrant that can only be issued by senior officials. And only if they think we have a one hundred percent chance of conviction, otherwise it could get seriously messy, we could blow the whole operation. Sad truth is even if we did send all of them down they would only set up shop somewhere else."

Danny cast his mind back to the beach and subsequently was asked to make a full statement the following day. Detective Sergeant Coburn was concerned for Danny's safety. He believed Danny was getting involved with some dangerous people; he stated his claim with assurance and laid the evidence before him. He told Danny how Ana had been involved with the gang and had been particularly close to Omar.

"You tried to help her, you did well, but you should back away now, forget about Ana and Omar, you can't do anything about it." Danny had explained the position he was in and Coburn agreed to help. The previous night they had a long conversation, they built a rapport and understanding, they shared fellowship.

"Danny I've done some digging like I promised, pulled in Peter Munday he's in Reading jail."

"Thanks."

~ ~ ~

Arthur sold knives and his extensive range was displayed in a glass cabinet and hung on the wall behind him in his dingy army surplus shop tucked under the railway arches in the less salubrious part of town. He wore the same style clothes as he sold off the peg and boasted to everybody that he was a battle hardened ex SAS soldier of fortune mercenary. A self-styled Rambo a legend in his own mind set.

When Danny entered the shop he was polishing the blade of a zombie knife with chainmail gloves.

"This is one serious fuck off knife," he said holding the weapon by the point of the blade and handle. He passed it over to Danny. Danny was conscious of a curious sensation which ran from his wrist and passed in a quivering tremor up his arm as he examined the knife.

"You can feel it can't you?" Arthur said. "Raw power." The blade was grooved and thick with two serrated edges razor sharp made of steel slightly twisted in a graceful curve. "Japanese. Just come in today, geezer said it was too big to slide down his pants kept thinking he would slice his nuts off."

A thin ray of light struck the blade from the opening door, specks of blood shone on the surface, a shiver ran down Danny's spine. Arthur had one eye on Danny and one eye on the customer who had just come through the door and was loitering round the back of the shop next to his array of army surplus jackets and trousers that were gathering dust under the glow of the one solitary light bulb that swung in the draft casting it's gloomy moving shadow over the garments.

The car wash was on the corner of the road opposite the park. Two brand new top of the range Jaguars were parked next to the office gleaming. Danny went over to have a closer look. All day Fayez made the lives of his sweated employees a misery to them. In his eyes they were a commodity, more like goats than people. Purchased for pennies, paid peanuts and kept as virtual prisoners in lock up garages sleeping ten to a mould infested room. Sleeping on the floor feet to head without the basic necessities, no hot running water and sharing a makeshift maggot infested kitchen and bathroom. Kept like animals for the sole purpose of making a profit for himself.

Every one of them was carefully selected; the better looking girls sent down the line to the brothel keepers and forced to sleep with up to ten men a day. Each had a past, a threatening dagger was hanging over their heads. Most were refugees, fugitives from justice or with no one to report them missing. Men women and children who had fled the war zones for the Promised Land and a better life. Some had crossed the channel on rubber boats, some on the backs of lorries, their names had been sent in advance by Omar's many agents and people smugglers across Europe and beyond.

It was a perfect system of slavery. They had paid thousands for safe passage handed to the gang before they landed and subsequently deducted from their slave wages. They would never pay back the money, the gang made sure of that.

~ ~ ~

"You alright my friend?"

"Good thanks"

"Cushty." He had deep set eyes, a shaved head and they called him Fayez.

"I prefer the red one," he said. "What do you want?"

In hindsight the question was innocent enough, his answer insufficient in light of the havoc it might cause. Danny told him everything about Ana and what he had learnt about the circumstances of her disappearance. Fayez told Danny that sometimes he was ashamed to tell people he was a Turkish Muslim, sometimes he told people he was Greek Cypriot instead. Most people couldn't tell the difference anyway everybody lumped us all together. He said he was sick to the stomach with all the bad press and negative stereotype. He said that people believed we were all bad all criminals. It wasn't true.

"Stop it with this nonsense. I am a very hard working man. I pay my taxes. Like with all countries, there are some that follows the law and some that play with it. Islamophobia is like a cancer in this country, it's propaganda to make all us Turks look like dirt. These people are not the true people, they are crazy and fucked up soldiers from the war."

It was a busy lunch time at the car wash. It was the weekend so the small crowded car park was tightly packed with customers having their cars washed by its legion of slave labour. After about ten seconds of uncomfortable silence which felt like an hour Fayez chuckled to himself.

"Ha funny just remembered something."

"What?"

"Come sit in car."

They got in. Fayez brushed a speck of dirt off his leather jacket and reached for a bottle of vodka which lay between his seat and the gear shift. He began swirling the dregs that remained at the bottom before quickly downing it, first checking for any unwanted observers.

"Something about this woman Ana, you ask. Three years ago I first met her. I remember she got very carried away pulling, biting, kicking me, trying to fight me off. I not notice smoke coming up from floor where I drop cigarette on my shirt, stupid. Room caught fire, Omar run in put out with fire, very angry with me, got out by skin on teeth how you say"

"Shame you didn't burn yourself down with the room," said Danny.

"I nearly did."

"Shame you didn't succeed."

"That is a nasty thing to say."

"You're a liar."

"Why you speak this?"

"Your tongue drips with poison. You're a rapist, a child rapist."

"Relax."

Fayez turned the key in the ignition and switched on the radio. Freddie Mercury's Bohemian Rhapsody blared out of the speakers.

Mama just killed a man, put my gun against his head, pulled the trigger now he's dead.

"You like the Queen? I know he is not a real man but he sings good."

"You're an evil paedophile all of you."

"You're wrong."

"Keeping those poor girls prisoners, getting them hooked on drugs, forcing them to sleep with men."

"Are you drunk? Why don't you shut up?"

Mama Mia Mama Mia Mama Mia Figaro, Beelzebub has a devil to decipher.

"You should be punished, go to prison, all of you. You should all fuck off back to where the hell you come from."

"You should shut up now before you say something you will regret, it must be very hard for you to understand what it is like to be a real man."

"What happened to Ana and that girl that went to the police? The one they found on the beach, did you kill her?"

"I can't say."

"Omar?"

Danny was getting nowhere so he pulled a knife. Danny grabbed him, put the knife to his throat and managed to pin him up against the car door.

Just wanna get out just wanna get right out of here.

"Start talking."
"W-wait."
"Yes."
"I-I…"
"You make no sense."
"I-."
"Speak English."
"Zena."
"Right."
"I, she died."
"Come on."
"You gonna to kill me you crazy?"
"Did you kill Zena?"
"Maybe."
"Ana?"
"What of this dumb whore?"
"What happened to her?"

"I don't know answer, she just go crazy bitch."
"Tell me?"
"She just disappear, go."

Nothing really matters. Anyone can see, nothing really matters to me, take me where the wind blows.

Fayez made a grab for the door handle. The door swung open. He fell out pulling Danny with him onto the forecourt; the knife fell under the car. Fayez kicked Danny hard in the testicles and quickly got up as Danny lay winded on the ground groaning.

"Shut up woman." Fayez said as Danny stopped groaning. "You really are crazy arsehole, you lucky man but you need keep your big mouth shut."

~ ~ ~

"Welcome everybody to the Wednesday night meeting of Alcoholics Anonymous, My name's Jim and I'm an alcoholic. This is an open meeting so anybody is allowed to attend. Joe has agreed to kick us off with the preamble. Joe."

"Hello I'm Joe and I'm a grateful recovering alcoholic" he said, then proceeded to read the preamble.

"Thank you Jim. I am delighted to introduce Kathy who has agreed to share this evening. Kathy."

"Hi everyone I'm Kathy and I'm an alcoholic. I would like to start by reading a small paragraph from the big book of Alcoholics Anonymous which is on page sixty two." She did it beautifully.

In her teens she was drinking, sniffing solvents, taking amphetamines, cannabis and ecstasy. She had trouble remembering most of it. She first tried heroin when she was in a women's prison aged twenty. It was easily smuggled in. Two years later, hopelessly addicted, she took up with a fellow junkie and moved to Bristol where he put her on the game. Pimping her out at fifty pounds an hour, but she had a hundred pound habit to feed.

She rolled up her sleeves to reveal her arms which were covered in track marks, she removed her false teeth. She said most of her teeth had fallen out, another effect of addiction. She also had a lot of knife scars from self-harming. She had been in and out of one co-dependent violent relationship after another. Estranged from her family for so long and deeply regretted the fact that she never saw her two daughters grow up, despite the fact they were now back in her life. But her biggest regret of all? She had a son and she didn't know where he was to this day.

Drinking and drugging all day everyday was the only way to stop the withdrawal symptoms. It was like banging herself repeatedly over the head with a hammer to stop the ache.

"It wasn't easy when I first came through the doors, but one day at a time, I haven't had a drink or drug in twelve years," she said.

"Thank you Kathy." A lot of people shared back, most people's stories were not as harrowing as Kathy's. Some people had never even been arrested for pissing in a graveyard. But it wasn't a competition everyone had reached their rock bottom. Then Danny spoke.

"I'm Danny and I am an alcoholic. I-I-I...." Danny tried to mouth the words but all he could do was stammer and choke on them. Tears welled up in his eyes. "I'm disgusting. I'm sick." Things started going through Danny's mind, thoughts that scared him and made him feel that he had to escape. Danny didn't even want to admit it to himself. He wanted to bury the memories deep inside himself, hoped they would never see the light of day. Danny had vowed he would take his secrets to the grave, but he couldn't escape them. Wherever he went he took his head with him. You're only as sick as your secrets. "I wish I was dead."

Danny didn't say much, neither did Tony. After the meeting they went in the back room and told each other more day to day events. Like a careful diary that the room recorded catalogues of things. Danny talked then Tony talked about what they thought on all subjects. Then Danny spoke about what was happening. Tony said that he had warned Danny time and time again not to get too involved, he said Danny was putting his life at risk and he didn't know what he was getting involved with yet. Danny knew the risks involved and he was fully prepared to make them.

"I really identified with what you shared, but you hear about people who top themselves all the time in my job. Young kids leaving their poor families behind, heartbroken. It's not fair, it's no joke, it's selfish. I wish I could detach myself from all the pain but I can't, you should never really say that stuff outside the rooms," Tony said.

"I have no one. They got killed, car accident. I was adopted but it's the same thing. I never knew my real mum or dad. My real mum got rid of me, didn't want to know. All I know was she was Lithuanian, don't even have a name. I think she was a drug addict, that's probably where I get it from."

"When's your birthday Danny?"

"Why, you gonna buy me a present?"

"When's your birthday?"

"First of May."

Coburn had been a detective for twenty years; he knew everything and nothing spooked him. Unfortunately they looked at the situation from opposite sides of the spectrum.

Tony was conditioned to do everything by the book. Danny was reckless and impatient.

"What's happening to this city?"

"We do manage to lock some people up occasionally."

"Tony, is Ana a sex slave?"

"There is a rumour, what do you think?"

"I really hope not."

"If I find out anything I will let you know."

"Likewise."

"Tony, why did you join the police?"

"Well to start with I suppose I wanted to stop all the mugging, raping and mindless violence."

"And have you managed to give it all up yet?"

~ ~ ~

Danny was struck by its familiarity and ordinariness but despite this he felt haunted. Something beyond the state of play affected his state of mind and motivation that he couldn't figure out. He walked down a dilapidated terrace street of empty units and flats many boarded up with graffiti-strewn metal shutters and ply board nailed to the windows. There was a black door between an Asian supermarket and a Polish shop, he rang the bell and someone let him in.

The lobby he entered was cramped. Danny spoke to the thickset mean looking man who frisked him, demanded fifty pounds then pushed him through a side door. Danny sat down and waited along a side wall. There were two three-seater sofas and a table with a selection of adult magazines. The interior door was continually opened and shut and guarded by two large men who never took their eyes off you.

A young man came through the door and sat down next to Danny. He was dressed all in black with bleached white cropped hair.

"I'm seeing Zora," he said. "Lots of girls in there but Zora's the best lovely she is, my little man's getting hard just thinking about it, who are you having?"

A young girl came through the door. She was a child really no more than fourteen. She was made up to look older than her tender years, flanked by two bigger men. The bleached man went into a room with her. Danny sat alone for ten minutes listening to the faint sounds of men groaning and children suffer. When another girl came in Danny shuddered as they went into the room. It was small and cramped with a double mattress on the floor. On a small table there was a box of condoms, some Vaseline and baby wipes. Nothing else.

"Ready?" she said. She looked soul destroyed.

"No."

"No?" She moved her hand between Danny's legs and began to unbuckle his belt but Danny edged away.

"What's wrong, don't you like me?"

"You're a child."

 "I seventeen."

"A child."

"Me no child." She started to undress.

"Stop, I don't want to do this."

"Why not, please I have to."

"Do you want to?"

"Doesn't matter." She kissed him, Danny recoiled.

"What is this, it's stupid you can't put dick in woman you man. I have to make you happy for Omar otherwise he angry."

"Don't worry about Omar, I will tell him you made me happy. You don't have to do this, you could run away, there are places and people that can help you."

"Omar give me drugs rape me. I good person why he rape me? This my body why he do this, I wish this person dead. I can't leave they find me bring me back, I prisoner. One girl leave tells the police, she dead." She started crying. "Sorry I cry, he speaks me I get you nice job in hotel, he lie to me."

"Where are your family?"

"I have no one. "

"How can I help you?"

"You can't."

"Anything just ask."

"Go don't come back."

The park is busy today. There are lots of customers outside the café buying coffee and hot dogs while it slowly pumped out cool jazz to everybody waiting in line, laughing and enjoying themselves. There were lots of babies in the park learning to walk. Danny watched them take a few steps then tumble over.

A group of Somalis were in the park sitting high up on the bank like a pack of hyenas stalking a victim or on the lookout for potential customers. They were all in their twenties. Danny could see them eyeing up local school girls, on occasions they would approach them, start chatting them up. The girls didn't like it very much and Danny wondered if there was something far more sinister going on.

The kids on the bikes arrive with the orders and the woman with the pram who hides the wraps under the baby.

The first of flaming June had lived up to its name as the hottest day of the year so far. The grey brick walls soaked up the full glare of the sun like a sponge and threw the heat back out again. Omar's begging gangs had set up in their positions outside the busiest shops and cash points displaying their cards. They had learnt the script by heart.

The regular beggars were looking for somewhere to escape from the heat. The cafes and pubs had moved their fold up chairs out onto the pavement continental style. The night was young, the atmosphere relaxed, later the fighting would start.

Danny walked along the market stalls, gazebos and tents stretched three thick on both sides of the main road, displaying produce and cheap knock off counterfeit merchandise. Behind the tents weaved an interlocking maze of passageways where traders sat on plastic chairs smoking and drinking and looking out for the local constabulary and market inspector. Small-time dealers were peddling weed sailing close to the wind as old drunks staggered past three sheets to that very same wind that chased through the maze of market stalls. This was the old-fashioned super information highway where deals were made and rumours spread and churned through the populace like the ever changing motion of the jet stream.

Some vendors were packing up for the day dismantling their stalls, as he reached the high street. Danny couldn't tell what he was supposed to be dressed up like, in a tiger onesie, jumping up and down in time with the perpetual thumping beat of his beatbox littered with expletives blaring out at full volume camped in the doorway of Marks and Spencer. Passing shoppers throwing money into his cap. It wasn't long until the enforcement officer took out his walkie-talkie and approached him, just as the manager of Marks and Spencer came outside and an argument erupted between the three.

Further down the street, a smart looking woman with tight fitting jeans and black T shirt was walking around with her laminated postcards. It showed a child in a hospital bed with all manner of tubes and pipes sticking out of her and attached to a heart monitor. She claimed it was her sick child and she needed to raise money for a private operation in America. Everybody giving, giving, giving, no wonder they never left this place but it was all a scam, a hoax a manipulation. Everything was just the same as usual. Except it wasn't.

~ ~ ~

Paddy wagons, police cars and ambulances moved silently through the city streets at the crack of dawn. Hand guns, truncheons and Tasers strapped to stab proof vests they sledgehammered through the side door.
    The guttural barks of Alsatians zigzagged from room to room. Picking up the scent of semen stained sheets, body odour and booze they slobbered up the staircase. Followed by the rumble of a dozen size tens thundering up the steps.
    A sticky soup of smell assaulting the senses. They burst through fast and furious fanning out in a protective film around the girls. Their bellows and barks blotted out the screams.
    A row of naked men spread-eagled and wall eyed against the wallpaper protested innocence. Man handled and manacled then marched out the door.

Detective Sergeant Coburn stood outside the police station In front of a bank of reporters. Cameras and flash bulbs whirling, microphones in his face.
    "Two years ago we made a solemn pledge to combat modern slavery by cracking down on criminal gangs who trafficked young women for sex. Police officers across our county took part in Operation Turk and raided dozens of properties in towns and cities across both counties that we believed were being used as illegal brothels.
    "Yesterday four women who are from the Middle East believed to be sex trafficking victims were rescued from a premises in the city. The victims include a fourteen year old girl from Albania and a seventeen year old girl from Syria. They were promised jobs in hotels, but instead

were forced into prostitution and had their passports and documents destroyed.

"They had all been subjected to serious sexual assaults by clients and traffickers. Officers raided a further three brothels in another county and detained ten Turkish nationals as part of a major investigation into organised crime.

"Working on information provided by the general public and tip offs from the local community, the police worked alongside the Home Office and immigration enforcement officers.

"Several warrants were executed, and a total of fifteen people were arrested and charged with operating an illegal brothel, kidnapping, false imprisonment, suspicion of rape, statutory rape, grievous bodily harm and possession and supply of controlled substances.

"Women and girls believed to be victims of sexual exploitation have been taken to a government safe house.

"Tackling organised crime is our primary priority. We were able to carry out raids because, over a period of time, we were able to build a precise picture of what was going on, thanks to information supplied by the general public and other agencies.

"The victims of sex trafficking are controlled in such a way that it is very difficult and rare for victims to give evidence. This can happen in any neighbourhood usually in unassuming rental properties which are leased for about six months and then moved somewhere else. Victims don't know how to get the help they do desperately need. There are often language difficulties and in some cases they may not even know they are being exploited and will be living in fear, having been brainwashed into a distrust of police and outside help. Due to the arrests made we have been successful in closing down a major drug dealing operation in the city which has caused death and misery to a large section of the community. Thank you."

~ ~ ~

The sombre song of the sea wailed in the dark uneasy like a company of shipwrecked souls holding colloquy among the waves as the rising sun tried to break through their wreck of broken cloud. The grey empty sea faintly visible as Ana withered and gibbered along the beach through the hissing hoary spray. Ana felt lost and alone with her memories casting her mind back.

The Serbian war machine was marching through the Balkans crushing everyone under their Jack boots. Tanks were ploughing through the forests destroying everything in their path. Jet fighters decimating towns and villages displacing thousands on the march. Burning down houses, raping women and children. Ethnic cleansing. Pushing back the resistance forces to the very edge of the borders until their dark malevolent shadow sat looming over the village poised for attack.

In the early years of the war in a small village sunk deep in the Bosnian hills young men and women tended their herds and flocks, ploughed the fields and scattered living the free life unaware of the impending storm yet to come.

She remembered those terrible years on the barbed wired battle scarred hills. Where the blood stained the earth and soaked through the mud to turn the ditch water red. She did her best to survive, kept herself alive as the corpses rotted and decayed in the unmarked graves all around her. Ana was on the edge of her sanity just hanging on by a long corroding thread that shot through her life.

Ana stepped over a barbed wire fence and into a field of horses. Twenty or more quiet and still stood grazing in the dunes by the edge of the sea huddled together for protection from the elements. Like silent white ghosts in a silent white world. She watched the breeze bluster over their backs and through their manes and tails. For a moment all time stood still. Then she heard a voice carried on the waves, the voice of Novak.

~ ~ ~

The dawn of a new June day was breaking as Danny walked briskly along the promenade that led eastwards towards the city. There were few folk about slopping down the prom battling against a strong south-westerly that had raged all night. Boats moored by the quay tossed and rolled on the backwash of the great breakers that swept by the pier head. Danny's stomach was rumbling like the sea when he sat down on the bench. He gazed across the sea and watched thick black smoke curl up through a ship's funnel pumping out toxic waste pollution into the atmosphere. Listened to the captain sound his horn a low deep sound that made him tremble inside. Where was she?

~ ~ ~

Ana began to walk into the sea. Plunged into complete darkness she sank beneath the icy surface. The water filled her lungs and she was taken down with the current which rolled and tossed her along the sea bed and spat her out to the surface. At the mercy of the sea she struggled to no avail. The swell rose, the waves grew higher. Choking on the vile waters the current span her around and churned her about and spat her to the surface. Rolling in the deep, swallowing the poison of the sea she sank like a stone. In the grip of imminent death she saw her past spreading through the bitter waves of the tempest. Churning through the pages of the wretched chronicles of her life as she floundered deeper into the slough. She saw slaughter and blood. Screaming victims herded from trains pushed down into pits toward blood soaked men. The flash of knives slitting throats, decapitated bodies. Naked women suspended on swinging chains by their ankles thrown into pits and tossed onto giant pyres rivers of blood flowing down the gutter. Images from the spawn of hell. Everything goes quiet an unfathomable peace in the fathoms and still she hears his voice and sees his face. "Come home you're safe now."

PART FIVE

Danny fished half a Mars Bar out of his coat pocket and held it out to the fox's gaping jaws. The fox snapped the chocolate from his hand, its slimy tongue tickling his fingers.

Early this morning the pavements had been strewn with litter, just as the morning before and the morning before, ad infinitum. As Danny pushed his cleaning trolley further down the road he saw a woman hunched over a bin looking for dog ends. As Danny walked towards her he offered her a cigarette. Danny didn't smoke himself but he often found packets with some left in them and kept them for people. Danny offered her one.

"It speaks," she said.

"Sorry."

"I'm surprised you have the intelligence to speak, sweeping up shit for a living," she hissed.

"It's a job."

"Don't talk to me, scum!"

Danny could tell she was from the local mental institution, it was only half mile away and the city was full of the unfortunates.

"Sorry," said Danny as she stared at him in a mentally disturbed manner.

As Danny turned and walked along the colonnade in front of the bus lanes the path became dirtier. The usual menagerie including plastic cups, cigarette butts, the odd Covid mask and laughing gas canisters.

Kevin sat in his usual spot with his placard which read 'No muny for fud plez help'. Kevin had been on the streets for four years but he was only twenty years old. He always sat reading a book although he couldn't actually read. He had severe dyslexia. Some people don't like to talk about how they wound up on the streets. It was just easier that way.

"Ok Boss," said Kevin.

Danny gave him a cigarette out of his packet. Kevin lit it and took a puff.

"Cheers dude," he said, smiling broadly, exposing his decaying teeth. Danny looked down at his shoes that were coming away from the soles and looked like they were talking.

"What size are you, ten? I found a nice pair of Nike boots yesterday I can bring them up the centre for you if you like?"

Danny was amazed what some people threw away. He was forever rescuing expensive coats, trousers and shoes out of dustbins. People would buy a new item and just dump the perfectly good off-cast in the rubbish. Danny would collect them all and keep them altogether in a storage cupboard at the depot. So if any of the homeless needed a new pair of shoes or a nice warm coat they knew who to ask.

Danny was providing a much needed service, he would take them up to the homeless shelter. He knew all the street people personally. He worked as a street cleaner now and had a place in a hostel but he was still part of their world and they looked up to him.

Danny spotted her down a narrow alley lying on the pavement barefoot drooling and shrouded in mist.

"Chloe!" Danny shouted. No response. He went up to her and knelt beside her. "Chloe?" Still no answer. The girl just lay on the ground unmoving drooling in delirium, possibly overdose. Danny took a bottle of water from his inside pocket. He lifted her chin and tried to pour water into her mouth but it just trickled out. He opened her mouth, tipped her head back and tried again. Then he poured the water over her head and tried again gently smoothing it into her hair like shampoo.

"This happens sometimes, don't worry. Wake up Chloe," he said.

She groaned. "I know I know."

Danny repeated the exercise holding her mouth open pouring the drink down her throat and wetting her hair with the water. "Come on two minutes."

"Uuuurgh!" Chloe coughed and sputtered, then spewed brown bile from her stomach, her eyes opened.

"What the fuck, oh it's you."

"I just saved your life again."

She became more alert and manoeuvred herself into an upright position and looked up at him."

"Fuck." Danny left her to recover.

Alexander Strauss, address no fixed abode, spent the whole day wandering around the city with his two bags for life poking through the ashtrays looking for doggies. His pockets were fit to burst.

Danny offered him a new cigarette he examined it.

"No like."

"Why not?"

"These taste better," he said, showing him the lipstick stained butts in his pockets.

"How about I find you a nice Havana, so long?" Danny demonstrated with his fingers apart and pretended to puff on the imaginary cigar.

"Like Winston Churchill," said Strauss. "Ok." They shook hands.

"See you later my friend," Strauss said whilst rooting through the bin.

Moving past Wilko, Rupert was sitting on his favourite bench clutching his heart and wheezing loudly. "Help me, help me please!" he called out. Most people ignored him; a few people stopped to see if he was alright, but then moved off swiftly.

As Danny got closer an attractive woman asked him if he was alright.

"Please please help me," Rupert said.

"What's the matter is it your heart, do you want me to call someone maybe an ambulance or a security guard?"

"Please sit down next to me I just want to talk to someone."

"I'm busy, I'm late for a meeting, do you actually want any help?"

"Please sit down and talk to me I'm so alone."

She looked flustered. "Sorry I can't help you." She moved off quickly.

Rupert wasn't homeless and you really couldn't accuse him of doing anything bad. He had a nice room in sheltered accommodation but he spent all day sitting on that bench because he had nothing else in his life. He didn't really have a bad heart, he was in good physical health. A big man with a huge curly mop of black hair and wore glasses with incredibly thick lenses so when you were close up to him his eyes looked enormous.

Past Pavarotti's on the corner Danny passed the blind man and his lover; they were both homeless and weighed down by heavy rucksacks struggling to get through the impatient hordes. Behind him was Brian who wandered around all day stroking a stuffed dog.

Danny's radio buzzed.

"26 are you receiving over?" said Control.

"Receiving go ahead over."
"Make your way to the public toilets and scrub some graffiti off the wall."
"Understood over."

Danny stood outside the public toilets with a mop, bucket and graffiti remover scrubbing some poetry off the wall.

>Jimmy didn't have a toilet in his flat
>So he had to crap on the living room mat
>The shit and the piss grew higher and higher
>And now it looks like a giant quagmire
>The neighbours complained of the dreadful smell
>As it seeped under the door and down the stairwell
>They said to the council this is absurd
>We keep slipping on poor Jimmy's turd
>So the council moved Jim to a posh bedsit
>So he could have a less disruptive shit
>But Jimmy missed all the fun of catching his
>Neighbours on the run
>So he wiped his bum on copies of the sun
>And posted them through their letter boxes
>One after one.

Danny saw two piglets walking towards him sweating in their stab vests.

"Just cleaning up after the phantom poet, messy bastard, he wants shooting," said Danny.

"Bit extreme," said PC Pinky.

"Anyway did you hear about Scottish Suzi?" said PC Perky."

"No not heard anything," Danny said.

"She's dead," said Perky.

"How?"

"Not sure overdose most likely."

"That's so sad," said Danny.

Max was floating around them sweating profusely in the mid-morning heat.

"Good riddance to bad rubbish, at least the toilets will be cleaner, she used to take her clients in there spunk and shit all over the place."

Perky frowned. "Any way perhaps you can help us?" as she took a piece of paper out of her folder which had a picture of an old lady that had gone missing.

"Have you seen this woman? She went missing from a nursing home a couple of days ago. She's got dementia, we're handing them out to anyone who might be able to help."

They both looked at the pictures but shook their heads.

"If you should see her call this number on the picture immediately, got to dash." They disappeared.

"God did you hear what they said about Suzi?" said Danny.

"I saw her only last Monday."

"Where?"

"None of your business."

"I'd just like to know, might be important."

"Fucks sake, in the toilets keeping her company, slapping her fat arse and watching it wiggle."

Danny watched Chloe creep up behind Max and put her hands over his eyes. She was still barefoot. Then she faced him.

"Who's this gorgeous bitch?" said Max.

"She's a nightmare," said Danny.

"Look at the beautiful dress you got me," Chloe said as she proceeded to look in Max's shopping bag. She pulled at a garment sticking out the bag, unfolded it and displayed it in front of the crowd.

"Dress," she said as she pulled out another, "and sexy knickers." She giggled.

"These are presents for my wife, a hundred quid these cost me." Max panted trying to stuff them back into his bag.

"No!" Chloe grabbed him by the arm and pulled him into the foyer of the public toilets.

"I can't talk for long, I'm with my wife," Max said.

His wife was hanging around. She looked like a bulldog chewing a wasp, a large lady with a fierce Italian temperament.

Chloe pulled herself next to Max and said, "I need some money."

"Ask Danny."

"He ain't got none please just ten quid."

"I haven't got anything, I spent it on the wife's presents."

"Please just ten quid, maybe twenty, I'll be nice to you."

Max pulled out a twenty from his back pocket and stuffed the money in the top of her T-shirt. Chloe took it out his hand, put it in her pocket, produced a radar key and dragged him with her into the disabled toilets.

Inside the toilet she kissed him gently on the lips. She then took his hands and pressed them gently against her breasts.

"Not in here," said Max.

"Shut up."

"But…"

"Shut it."

She moved her hands down his front and kissed him on the mouth moving her tongue around inside his lips. She kissed his eyelids his ears and his neck moved her hand between his legs and squeezed.

Max groaned.

"Ssssh quiet."

The old man's heart was hammering and he felt a swelling in his pants and she had a look of lust on her face.

"Don't worry." She squeezed him again.

"The wife's …"

"Don't matter."

"Look what you've done to me," he said and showed her the bulge of his erection under his trousers.

"Cunt," Chloe snarled venomously. "Old cunt." Then she looked at him dreamily, pushed him up against the wall and started to unbuckle his belt, pulled his trousers down and squeezed him again.

"Stop, the wife."

She stopped and looked at him with disgust. "Cunt, dirty old cunt."

Max started to tidy himself up. Then Chloe pushed against the wall started undoing his belt pulled down his trousers, pants again she squeezed him and pinned him against the wall. She gave him a long hard psychopathic glare, put her hand around his throat and started to throttle him.

"Rape! Rape!" she started to scream then there was a bang at the door. She let go. Someone opened the door.

Max stood there frozen; he didn't know what to do. Now there was a lot of concern flying around. Max was concerned about what he was going to do next. Chloe was concerned about what she was going to do next. But no one was more concerned than the old man with his walking frame who came in to see them both standing in front of him with his trousers and pants around his ankles and her clutching his testicles and began shuffling backwards apologetically.

With the door wide open Max could see his wife moving towards him. Chloe scarpered.

"What you doing with that a woman!"

"What woman?"

"I gotta eyes I a see her."

His wife was mean, scary, built like a rhino with flaming nostrils. She practically pulled him off his feet and dragged him out of the cubicle.

Tea break. Suddenly it came speeding out of nowhere scattering the crowd, startled by the screech of brakes, Danny froze in the path of the mobility scooter. He tensed every muscle in his body, waiting for the final impact. The driver slammed on his brakes hard and stopped two inches in front of him.

"Oh I've got some terrible news about our Alf," he said. "Fell through a trap door and broke his neck."

"Oh God that's terrible, was he doing renovations?"

"No, they were hanging him, huh," said Tommy, he was a proper comedian. His real name was Ian, but everyone called him Tommy on account of the fact that he reminded everyone of Tommy Steele. He was a dead ringer.

"Just seen that girl of yours Chloe pissed out of her head yelling and screaming at someone. You've got big problems mate wouldn't want to be in your shoes."

"She's not my girlfriend."

"I know she must have had the baby, what colour, was it green?"

"No."

"I know that, I mean what colour black or white?"

"Can't really tell."

"Must have been that Turkish bloke she was knocking around with."

"Maybe, where is it?"

"They're gonna put him in foster care. She's allowed to visit but they've got her jumping through hoops. She's got to sort herself out. They're gonna drug test her regular so she's got to stay clean if she gets in trouble with the law again."

"Sounds like Ana. I admire you for what you did for her. You tried to help but I'll think you're an idiot if you get involved with another one. You'll have hell to pay. I won't judge you, do what the hell you like but she will put you through hell. I know what I'm talking about. My wife she was a whore and a drunk. Stuck with her twenty years. Gotta go." Tommy swiftly moved off sounding his hooter.

Danny was in the high street chatting to the regulars all the broken lonely hearted souls. They all had their stories to tell. Sweeping around the corner he saw Philip licking the inside of a cake bar he had just fished out the bin. Phil had been on the streets twenty five years. Nobody knew much about him; he kept himself to himself. He didn't go up the centre, he just spent all day lying on the bench or being sick. It was a miracle he wasn't dead; it was a miracle half the street people weren't dead. I suppose there weren't many viruses that could survive in his dirty veins.

Four people slept outside McDonald's. These four hadn't been in the city very long. A lot of homeless live a transient lifestyle and one day they all turned up together. They began living rough up north, then they moved to the Midlands and slowly worked themselves south until they got here. They were all in their twenties heavy drinkers and drug users. They got into some heavy bother with some dealers so they came here to escape. They told Danny that one day they jumped a dealer in Manchester and stole all his gear and money. So they had to escape in case of reprisals. They were forever looking over their shoulders.

The girls from the church were approaching. Magda and her company. Suddenly their conversation stopped as they started to hand out food packages and cups of tea.

Next door neighbour Stellica sat drinking a cup of tea in the doorway of Marks and Spencer. He always kept his doorway nice and clean, which was more than could be said for the others, who always left their cardboard cups of urine, empty food wrappers and the occasional syringe. Which Danny had to deal with very carefully and dispose of in a yellow sharps box.

"Morning Stell. Do you want me to chuck your wet cardboard away? I can get you some more," asked Danny.

"It's ok I don't need cardboard."

"No cardboard?"

"I was in military I'm used to this, people very generous giving me money I don't ask not so bad I don't have to pay money for board and lodging."

"Why don't you get a tent and live up camp?"

"People steal my stuff, you can't trust anyone up the camp."

"You need anything?"

"No I don't need your money, I have enough no pay bills or rent I am free."

"Free?"

"I had flat, didn't like it feels like animal in cage. This is simple. I go soon London, start job construction I know London they have room for me."

"Great." Danny picked up his wet cardboard, put it in his cleaning trolley and headed through the arcade. Danny saw a man standing next to a bin unzip his flies and started to urinate up the wall. He wasn't shy about it, he pulled out his plonker and shook it about oblivious. A passing girl had a look of abject horror on her face. Danny was going to have to use the scrubbing brush and disinfectant.

"Hi baby," said Chloe. Danny stopped scrubbing and lent the brush against the wall. She stood arm in arm with some man he had never seen before who stood jerking all over the place and beaming ear to ear.

"Hot last night, where are you staying at the moment?" asked Danny.

"With Jack."

Jack grinned. Danny gave a sigh of relief. He didn't much care who she stayed with but it was safer off the streets for a woman. Then she gave him a massive hug squeezing his whole body in a vice like grip. She was pressing so hard against him it activated the transmission switch on his radio. Wherever anyone happened to be on site every guard and every cleaner heard. "Love you baby."

Danny heard a lot of sniggering on his radio from the control room.

"Go again last caller," Control said.

"Nothing over" said Danny.

"Oh I thought you said you loved me over "

"No."

"Why what's wrong with me?"

"Hey."

There was a lot of laughter coming from the control room.

"I stayed with Jack last night. Sex for rent, but he couldn't manage it, tiny dick." Jack stopped smiling.

"I spent all my money on the kid, can I borrow five quid?" she asked.

"Why not?" Danny put his hand in his back pocket and gave her the dosh. He was a soft touch.

"I've got to go to court next week. How am I getting to court no cunt will give me money for the ticket it's miles away and I don't know the train times."

She took out the letter from probation; it had a map attached with directions of how to get there, the hearing dates and times. It was early she would need to catch a train and maybe a bus as well.

"Can you lend me the dosh I spent it all on the kid's birthday fuck sake. Can you come with me?"

"I will have to work, can't you go with someone from the centre?"

"Got banned, won't help me anymore."

"What about the Salvation?"

"Got banned."

"What? The Sally don't ban people."

"They found spice in me locker."

"Ok I'll go with you. Take the day off."

"And pay for the ticket?"

"Yes alright," Danny said and he was sure he heard her mutter 'stupid cunt' under her breath when she went.

Danny finished scrubbing the urine off the ground and continued on his route when he spotted a man smoking next to a non-smoking sign. Usually he kept his mouth shut. But on this occasion he risked it.

"Sorry mate. No smoking, if you get caught you might get fined just trying to help." He looked at Danny as if he was shit on his shoes.

"Don't you know who I am?" he said. "I'm the king of this town I am, I own these streets nobody's allowed round here unless I say so I rule these streets I do." He stood next to Danny with his green baseball cap turned sideways, his large beer gut hanging from underneath his torn T shirt. "I own this place I do."

"What's your name?" asked Danny.

"Don't ask me my name in public unless you wanna get shanked." Then he gave Danny a gentle shove and threw the lighted cigarette in the bin. Instinctively Danny grabbed the bin key, pulled out the liner, tipped the contents of the rubbish on the ground and stamped out the fire. As he was replacing a fresh bin liner he saw a group of about ten travellers shuffling about outside the Sports Direct with bags full of sports clothing and bits and pieces. Two of whose arms and necks were red raw, with wavy lines.

Danny read about it in the paper, they were attacked in the park. Some kid on a mountain bike threw hydrochloric acid at them then bolted off. Retribution had been served from a dealer that they double crossed, descriptions were vague.

Danny could hear the bearded lady shouting she hadn't taken her meds and was telling everyone to fuck off. Out of the corner of his eye he saw Bernice in his high heels, black fishnet stockings and a size twenty dress stretched to split over his bulging muscles, make up smeared all over his face, staggering about like a drunken cart horse. Someone wolf whistled.

Danny finished changing the bin outside the sports shop and wiped the stains off the side. He saw Kevin hanging around begging for money. "Excuse me, can you spare us some change please Sir or Madam." He wasn't aggressive in his manner and when they declined he wished them a nice day. Kevin didn't steal from shops, he just hung around outside them. He was a tragic individual who shifted around the town all day, being moved constantly from place to place. He would beg until he had enough money for his fix. Then he would disappear to meet his dealer, then go to the council toilet or somewhere quiet, inject himself. Then a few hours later he would come back and inject some more.

He just begged, it was a vicious cycle he was always too stoned to steal and couldn't run for toffee. His body had become weak and feeble. Danny didn't think he had long left in this world. His sadness was not planned. The road he went down was grey empty and without end.

"Morning Kev."

"Morning Boss." Danny gave him four cigarettes he found in a packet out the bin. "Here you are."

"Thank you." Kevin was always grateful for anything he could get.

"Don't forget to eat."

Kevin should be suffering from every disease known to human science. Piles from sitting on cold hard pavements, rickets from a lifelong diet of cola and chips. Aids from sharing needles, hepatitis A, B and C from all the shit that he had swallowed. Probably the bubonic plague from lying in rat infested sewer squats. Abscesses in the gums from never brushing his teeth but he looked healthy enough.

The traveller community were back in force with their teardrop tattoos and swagger. They had their other halves with them and they were giving it large. Swearing and spitting on the ground, and that was just the women. The babies were in huge prams like royal carriages, flashy and over the top being paraded around. Big Aaron pulled a wad of bank notes out his pocket and gave it to his wife. As she pushed the baby into Tesco Kevin shuffled over and he took him to one side and made a crafty exchange.

Danny's radio clicked. "Attention all call signs we have a report of a stolen bicycle being ridden on site. IC 1 male black hair wearing a green tracksuit be aware over."

Outside Primark a police car had pulled up and Danny saw two policemen helping a woman into the back. She wasn't struggling. A shop guard was with her pushing a pram. A WPC was with them holding a baby. The guard put the pram in the back and they drove away.

"Fuck off, fuck off out of it, fuck off out the way." The man in the green tracksuit was wobbling about all over the place trying to ride the bike throughout the crowded arcade.

Danny's radio clicked. "Kilo 10 just heading past Primark now see if you can block his path." Danny heard the guard panting on the other end of the line.

"Where is he?"

"Just gone down station passage… You can cut him off if you're quick."

"I can't see him."

"Just turned left heading to bus station."

All Danny could hear was a lot of panting and voices echoing down the wires.

"Turned back into the precinct going down Punch Lane." Panting like an Alsatian, a guard ran straight past Danny. The man on the bike was heading towards him but he swerved right passed him.

"Fuck off out the way."

"Done a left into the bus station."

He was going around in circles. Anticipating his next move, Danny turned his trolley around and headed to Punch Lane, turning the corner he could see him peddling erratically towards him.

"Danny block his path, block his path!"

Danny ran into his path with the trolley. He was trying to avoid him swinging left and right. Danny pushed his trolley into the front wheels, he skidded and the back wheel slid out. The thief tried to steady himself with his feet but Danny grabbed the back of the bike. The thief tried to swipe Danny but he ducked then the guard caught up and grabbed him and held on wheezing.

"Control suspect apre. Apprehend over."

~ ~ ~

Lunch break. Danny was starving so he decided to get some fish and chips inside him. Inside he ran into Brian. Brian was an embarrassment; the expression 'you can't take him anywhere' was made for him. He had a unique talent for putting his foot in it and saying precisely the wrong thing at precisely the wrong time.

It was a busy time at the city fish bar, it was the holidays so the small crowded hot room opposite the counter was packed tightly with mums, dads and children.

The smell of fish and chips frying filled the air, as Danny looked at the huge menu board trying to decide what to have. Cod, plaice, haddock or maybe skate. He had never had skate. Brian was doing his usual thing, eyeing up any half decent looking woman under fifty. He wasn't subtle about it. They were about fourth or fifth in the queue when Danny asked the question.

"Do you like skate, what's it like? I've never had it."

It was an innocent enough question but the answer was unexpected even by Brian's standards.

In his loud booming voice he blurted out, "Did you know the inside of a skate is exactly like a woman's fanny?"

Danny just wanted the ground to open up beneath him and swallow him up. There was a ripple of discord and accusing looks. But it was too late; he wished he had kept his mouth shut.

"A fisherman told me that on long fishing trips, they used to wrap the skate around their cocks and masturbate," Brian said.

Danny felt rooted to the spot. He heard one snigger but not much else. The woman behind the fish bar gave him a funny look. Danny just smiled embarrassingly. Brian would always find the loosest connection to some filth. Eventually they got served and got out. They didn't sell much skate lunchtime.

"26 are you receiving over?"

"26 received go ahead."

"Could you make your way to Burger King please need your help over."

Danny got to Burger King in five minutes. Inside were most of the rough sleepers who had been banned from McDonald's across the street. John was sat in the corner with his rucksack and guitar case on the floor. He was talking to Richard. Danny didn't know Richard very well, he didn't go up the centre, some people just didn't. Some people don't like to, various reasons, too many rules, too many undesirables or just plain old fashioned pride.

Richard was a good artist. He painted pictures and sold them to the tourists. He's got a big portfolio and he was even given a small exhibition once at the local library after the paper did an article about him. They usually went to Caffé Nero but they were worried about the recent stories.

Danny strolled up to the counter.

"Just a coffee please milk no faeces."

"Pardon?"

"Just a coffee please."

Spike was leaning against the counter, his clothes, hands and face were filthy covered in mud and dirt. He had a new haircut or at least it looked like he had tried to cut it himself without a mirror. He put a cardboard crown on his head to cover the damage and had two straws stuck up his nose. He didn't know what planet he was on. He went and sat down with the scrawny little man in the corner who had been staring at his cup of coffee for the last thirty minutes. The man who nobody spoke to, the man with no ears.

Danny remembered the day he walked into the centre and saw that strange new man with half his ears chopped off. Twenty percent of rough sleepers had spent time inside at one point or another, so they knew the signs. They figured it out. Danny remembered the night they decided to approach him about it. A few of them were sitting on the steps outside the Superdrug store. They just asked him flat out. "Are you a paedophile?" He was very matter of fact about it. He had no shame, felt no guilt or remorse. He told them all the gory details revelled in his notoriety. I will spare you.

Danny told the security about him as they didn't know. He told them that he wished he didn't know all these dangerous people. They told him they were glad he did. Danny knew a lot of things they didn't, he was a useful source of information when necessary. Security followed Steve with the cameras constantly. They even had two guards on twenty four hour Steve watch. They even followed him into the lavatories when he took a slash. Steve quite enjoyed his notoriety in a sick and twisted kind of way.

Danny could hear a lot of commotion coming from somewhere. There was shouting coming from upstairs and he recognised the voice.

"Your colleagues are upstairs," Abigail said.

Danny grabbed his coffee and went up. Through the door he was met with the sight of Maria standing on the table screaming her head off at the manager and two security guards.

"You have to pay," the manager demanded.

"No why explain my person?"

"You have to pay for the food."

"No, this place shit, no money this place dirty infections."

Her accent to Danny was like a knife in the heart. Bosnia. Ana was never far from his thoughts. Maria and Ana were friends, all three knew each other. Security usually called Danny to help if they knew him.

She saw Danny.

"Hey Danny. No Premier Inn no hotel they don't like me stay."

"No hotel."

"Send me back camp."

"Have you got any money?" Danny asked. He was fully prepared to pay for the stolen items and put an end to proceedings.

"Kevin stole my money. Kevin, yes you deaf? Kevin stole my money and my clothes."

"Why?"

"No hotel no money sleep in street."

The manager was looking very perturbed and hassled. He kept looking at his watch and there was nobody else upstairs.

"Look I haven't got time for this can you please help me sort this out. I am very sorry but I'm sick of you people causing problems."

Danny heard two more familiar voices behind him and saw two more sweating security guards come in.

"Surprise! Why you so fat too much eat go diet more exercise."

"We get enough exercise chasing you around all day," one said.

"Maria get off the table we haven't got time for this."

"Dickhead."

"Thanks."

"Slap me."

"No I don't want to slap you."

"Why you man?"

"Real men don't hit women Maria."

"Bullshit." Maria wasn't playing ball, she wasn't paying and she wasn't going.

"Are you going to get off the table or are we going to have to call 126?"

Papa 126 was well known to Maria, they didn't like each other.

"126 Dickhead, 457 Dickhead."

The guard spoke into his radio. "Control you haven't seen 126 parked up anywhere have you, have you seen anyone available over?"

"I called the police an hour ago," said the manager.

"One second I need pee pee."

Maria squatted and moved her knickers to the side. They smelt a pungent odour and watched the floor beneath her flood with hot yellow steaming liquid, as she pissed all over the table. It ran off the sides slowly dripping to the floor.

"You want locking up," said the manager, just as 126 burst through the door and glared at her.

"Surprise."

"Are we going to do this the easy way or the hard way?" 126 said.

"You arrest me," she said as 126 took out the cuffs.

"Yes."

"Maybe one night in cells. Maybe dinner, me no dinner. Me ban from shelter, me ban from Salvation Army."

"Is there anywhere you're not banned?"

She had to think, then she replied. "Eer, here?"

126 looked around at everyone, then back at Maria, then back at the puddle of urine on the floor which was creeping everywhere closer towards their toes, so they shuffled back.

"I think you can safely add this place to the list."

"Okie dokie dick head." Maria jumped off the table and held out her wrists. "You cuff me."

"No need if you come quietly."

She kissed Danny and left.

It was coming to the end of a long day when Danny got a call on his radio.

"Control to 26 can you go into the west yard and sweep up some rubbish the wind has knocked a bin over and it's gone everywhere."

"Received."

The wind had started to gust and the litter was flying all over the place. There was no point in chasing it around. Danny went into the west yard and could see that one of the large wheelie bins had blown over. Paper bags were flying all around him.

Clutching a large bin bag he started grabbing the rubbish out of the air and plucking it off the ground, cramming it into the sack. Large plastic bags were flying through the air and whizzing around like mini twisters. Flying over parked cars, landing on the windscreens and getting lodged under the tyres.

The yard backed onto some shops and each unit had its individual bin. The hairdresser's bin had blown over as had the clothes shop's. The bags were not tied up so all the hair had spilt and strands were blowing over the yard. It was impossible. Most of the rubbish was blowing towards the metal gate which led to a secluded bin yard.

Danny went through the gate and opened the bins and started shovelling the rubbish inside. That's when he saw it.

Why do people always scream in films when they see a dead body? It wasn't Danny's natural reaction. His whole body stiffened and he didn't have the breath in him to even speak watching rubbish blow over the body. Numb with shock he pressed the transmission on his radio but he didn't speak. Then he chuckled to himself it was just Kevin. Danny gave him a gentle kick to the side. He stirred and moaned.

"You okay?"

"Yes boss." He was fine.

Danny crossed the street and headed to Smyth's. Jamie was standing outside selling the Big Issue. He had a permanently blocked nose and always sounded like he had a cold asking for a tissue. "Big tissue please. Big tissue please."

This week the cover had a picture of a ginger tom cat on the cover. 'A street cat named Bob'

"How's it going?" Danny asked him.

"Not bad only been here two hours but the reason I think it's selling so quick is 'cause it's got a picture of a soppy cat on the cover."

"Have you seen the film?"

"No."

"Read the book?"

"A bit of it."

"What you think?"

"It's a sweet enough story, not very realistic though."

"Well it's for kids, they probably only bought it for the cat picture."

"People love soppy cats, the internet has millions of videos of 'em, billions of hits."

A woman interrupted their conversation and bought a copy.

"It must be true," said Danny.

"Fair enough, you can't really tell the truth in a film. Nobody wants to watch a film or read a book about what really happens on the street. No one wants to see a kid taking it up the dirt box for a packet of skunk, getting the crap kicked out of him and waking up with his face in a puddle of sick. Put you right off your popcorn."

Jamie was a bit camp in his mannerisms. Danny suspected it was the artist in him.

Danny's radio buzzed. "Control to 26 can you go to the public toilets and scrub Wordsworth's latest ode off the wall?"

"Received."

Outside the toilet a youth was sitting with his back against the wall bombed out of his skull on skunk weed. Pale as a ghost with his eyes blacked up with mascara. "Got any weed?" he said.

A heavy set man very unsteady on his feet staggered out of the toilet towards Danny, nearly knocked him over then threw up on the pavement slightly splashing Danny's work boots. Great, more pavement pizza to clean up, thought Danny.

Wordsworth's latest epic was written on the cubicle door in black spray paint.

> In days of old, when knights were bold
> And johnnies weren't invented
> They grabbed a sock and tied a knot
> And fucked away contented.

As Danny was cleaning it off he spotted something on the ground. On first impression it looked like a tea bag. He held it up so he could see it more clearly. It was about the size of a tea bag. A brown powdery substance in a muslin package broken at one end. Danny put it in his pocket and went outside, began scrubbing the vomit down the drain.

Pavel was lying face down on the ground scrabbling about on all fours. He lifted himself up dragging his trousers over his knees in the process but he wasn't wearing underwear revealing all. Rupert sat rocking back and forth on his bench clutching his heart and wheezing and across the streets some school kids were chucking their chips at a man in a wheelchair. Everything was normal.

He took the package over to Stellica who was outside Marks and Spencer and showed it to him.

"Do you know what this is?" Danny asked him. He glanced at it then studied it more closely.

"Heroin."

"You sure? Bit of a funny colour."

"I been on the streets long enough to recognise this shit. Brown, white, fifty shades of grey take your pick."

Danny walked a bit further along the road, lent against the wall then radioed Control.

"26 to Control, I've found a bag of heroin, what should I do with it, over?"

"Where did you find it?"

"Toilet floor."

"Bring it up to Control over."

Upstairs in the control room Ted sat staring at a wall of monitors. One hundred and fifty cameras which covered the shopping centre and received live feeds from other cameras across the city. Danny gave him the package.

"It's not a tea bag," Danny said.

Ted sniffed it, held it up to the light then wrapped it up in a plastic bag, labelled it and put it in the draw.

"Cheers mate I'll smoke it later," he replied then he zoomed in on one of the cameras to a woman sitting on a bench outside the Clock Tower. "Your friend."

Danny took a closer look and saw Chloe.

"Be careful mate. You still in that hostel?"

"Yes."

"How long you been sober now?"

"Just for Today."

"Oh I get it."

"You got next week off haven't you... Going to visit that bastard in prison?"

"Yes."

"Look Danny..."

"What?"

"Nothing."

"Any news about Ana?" He changed the subject.

"I dunno where she's gone."

"Sorry I know you two were really close."

"What happened to the baby?"

"Adoption."

"Boy or girl?"

"Boy, ginger, lots of ginger hair."

"Ah could of been Prince Harry then."

Danny chuckled with tears in his eyes. "Could have been you," he said.

Danny chatted with Ted a while before he knocked off. Ted needed a break from looking at the cameras. Danny asked him what the funniest thing he ever saw was. He said most of the funny stuff happened at night and showed him a few burns.

~ ~ ~

Danny strode across the square. Sound waves from holes drilled in exhaust pipes intercepted by high pitched security alarms shuddered the still air. The last of the drunks and derelicts left their begging spots and sloped back to their tents and squats.

The sun was descending into a red ditch of clouds turning the sky to a blanket of purple haze that ran south towards the sea. The Clock Tower chimed its quarter like it had in centuries past, cajoling Danny to increase his speed, as he trudged down the street that sloped towards Chloe.

Brown speckled scruffy feathered juveniles that had fallen from low hanging roof top nests, screeched for their parents that swooped and dive-bombed overhead, as they fought over thrown out scraps of bread and bowls of water.

The sun sank lower, paler and mellow, softening the sharp outlines and edges of trees and buildings. Falling into a gap on the horizon like a solstice, it flooded a river of light towards him. Stretching the shadows and silhouettes into deep velvety black.

Standing before her dazzled by the light, she raised her hand to her eyes. Danny must have loomed like a phantom before her.

"My clothes stink," said Chloe. "Can I borrow your washing machine?"

"Can't you take it up the…?" Banned, Danny remembered. "Ok what you going to wear?"

Chloe shrugged. Keeping clean on the streets was hard enough but when everyone had abandoned you rightly or wrongly it was impossible.

"Hang on, hasn't Jack got one?"

"Left Jack."

"You still got that old tent?"

"Someone nicked it "

"Really… You ain't bullshitting me are you?" A man sat next to her talking to himself oblivious to the conversation as people pushed past on their journeys.

"Can't I stay round yours?"

"Not allowed."

"Please just one night wash me clothes then fuck off, maybe a shower bit of breakfast."

"Don't push it."

"I'll be nice to you."

"No need for that. One night but you can't tell anyone. No drugs, I can't risk it. If anyone catches you I'm out on the streets again."

"I promise."

"Meet me at nine o'clock here."

"Can't we go now?"

"I've got a meeting. See you at nine."

~ ~ ~

The group of men and women were shuffling around outside the church door, armed with mobiles throwing moving beams of light across the porch door. Father Dylan stood leaning far too close to sister Josephine. Danny passed them all and went inside. Just inside the door was a table spread with tea, coffee and biscuits. Danny poured himself a coffee and took a Kit Kat.

In the adjacent room all the tables and chairs had been pushed together. The lights were flicked and the room shone brilliantly, the chairs set along the sides began to fill up.

Joe sat next to the door. A known trouble maker, serial shoplifter and drug addict. He was all over City Watch radio and every time he came onto the shopping centre security had to drag him away. In fact most of the people in the room caused trouble at the shopping centre.

Next to him sat John. John had recently been released from prison and was currently on bail for alleged assault and battery. He had been diagnosed with borderline personality disorder and needed help to break away from his cycle of prison, street drugs, violence, prison.

Kelly sat opposite, a beautiful girl once about thirty drug addict and prostitute. She was sent to prison a month ago for shoplifting and she had just been released. She's been on the streets for five years. A long history of heroin abuse having first used when she was fourteen. She's currently on meth. She wants to get clean. She's lost count of how many times she's been inside but it's most of her adult life. She's scared to stop using and unable to without secure accommodation.

She claims she's better able to cope inside than out. She wants a place at a treatment centre but has been told she can't due to not engaging with support services in the past. She has been diagnosed with schizophrenia, bipolar, substance abuse, psychosis and even labelled a psychopath. Besides her other drugs she is on a daily prescription of Diazepam, Paroxetine, Quetiapine and Denzapine. She rattled when she walked.

Martin sat next to her. He has been a heroin and crack user on and off for twenty years. He was clean once for five years but has been in and out of prison since he was sixteen. He's been using since he was twenty. He says it keeps him warm at night and is his preferred choice of painkiller.

Martin got out of prison six months ago after serving a sentence for ABH and is looking for a return ticket. It won't take him long to find one. He likes prison and his friends are there. He had three square meals a day and a roof over his head. Which is more than he has here.

Recently a man stabbed a complete stranger to death in the subway because he just wanted to go back inside. He had a reputation in jail. He was respected, feared even. On the outside he felt insignificant and unable to cope.

Thomas sat on the floor, he was given a fifty day prison sentence for breach of probation. He served forty, on the day of his release he overdosed on spice. He has always committed drug related crime. But says if he could keep clean he would stop fucking about. He is on anti-psychotics and mood stabilisers. He also has a split personality disorder. He self-harms all the time and has cuts all over his wrists and arms. He says it gives him release and proof of existence.

Danny looked around at everyone waiting for the meeting to start. He had the longest sobriety in the room today. He was just as bad as them once, he's getting better one day at a time. But the program only works for people that want it, not for people that need it.

Simone was playing table tennis with Harry. Keith was lounging on the easy chair stroking his white boxer dog. Keith always reminded Danny of a character out of Charles Dickens with his diminutive stature and faithful boxer. Most people had dogs for companionship and protection. Some people might think it cruel but the dogs were well fed and looked after and it earned you twice as much begging.

The ping pong ball flew off the table and bounced down the room it settled between Fred's feet who was still ranting about the aliens to anyone unfortunate enough to find themselves sitting next to him.

"The Queen and the Duke of Edinburgh were shapeshifters who drank human blood to look like us. They were both giant lizards," he yelled. Harry had to crawl under the table to collect the ball which had rolled under Kevin's feet. He was trying on the boots Danny had found him. "Thanks for the boots," he shouted.

Sam and Joe were back at the centre; they had been housed three months ago but were back living rough again. Some people who did live on the streets went to visit their families sometimes and their families didn't even know they were living rough. Pride can make you do strange things. People would lie to their parents or children. They would pretend they were working overseas and had a job, rather than admit they had lost everything and living in a tent in the woods.

Some people had been lying to their family for years and some people found it hard to adjust to a normal life. They couldn't cope with living in a flat. They missed their friends, forgot to pay the bills or accidentally burnt the place down.

Garry was putting up a new poster on the notice board. John was going into hospital and needed someone to look after his dog. Then he sat down at the table.

"Hello I'm Danny and I am a recovering alcoholic."

"Hello Danny," they all replied.

"I'll keep it short. It says on my little plastic sobriety chip 'to thy own self be true'. That doesn't mean I can be honest with myself and bullshit everyone else. Honesty, open mindedness and wisdom are the keystones to my recovery. They are indispensable. Drinking and lying went hand in hand with me. It's part of the illness. Both equally destructive afflictions which fed off each other. I was never happy in my own skin and used drink to purge myself so I didn't have to feel anymore. But it didn't work in the end. Just put me in a downward spiral which in the end led to incomprehensible demoralisation. But thanks to AA and the program of recovery I have been able to keep sober and I know I can stay sober. Thanks for listening."

~ ~ ~

Chloe wasn't waiting at the Clock Tower when he got there so he went straight home. When he got back home Chloe was watching the television slumped in his armchair with half a bottle of vodka on her lap. She was on the phone. She knew his address. She must have sweet talked herself in and used the spare key he hid under the plant pot.

"Hey Carlos, what you doing, come over Danny's gaff seven seagulls house, bring ye gear, sleep over come on, air con."

"Who are you calling?"

"Shut it." She dialled again. "What, yes Danny's gaff."

There was a knock at the door. "Hang on." She put the phone down and answered the door. "Alright mate sit your arses daan."

A man and a woman in their twenties came in loaded down with rucksacks. "Got any weed?" he said. She gave them both a kiss and they came in.

"Relax sit daan, TV, shower," Chloe said. The two came in and walked around Danny's flat sheepishly.

"This where we staying?" said the girl. Chloe gave Danny a sly glance

"Sshh," she said. "This your boyfriend, he's nice." Chloe passed the girl the bottle of vodka.

"When you gonna tell us what we have to say?" The girl asked Chloe quietly but not quietly enough.

"Sshh." Chloe looked guiltily at Danny.

"This is nice, thanks for letting us stay," the girl said.

"You look a mess," she said to the boyfriend.

"I need go wash meself and change," he said. He went into Danny's shower room while the other two sat down on Danny's bed smoking, drinking and talking.

Danny felt strangely disconnected from all this unexpected behaviour like it really wasn't happening; he was having the strangest thoughts.

"Don't look so worried, they're nice people," Chloe said. Danny walked into his kitchen area and poured himself a glass of water. He stood there drinking and looking out of the window across the rooftops of buildings out over towards the sea. Then he heard a strange noise coming from the shower room, so he opened the door and saw the boyfriend sitting on the toilet about to stick a needle in his arm.

"What you looking at?"

"Get out get out now."

"Cunt."

"Get…"

"Ok don't piss your knickers love."

Danny lifted him off the toilet seat and they stood nose to nose. He just smiled at Danny. Danny grabbed his shirt, twisted him around and pushed him out. Then he heard a smash. He turned round and saw the girl kneeling on the floor. She had smashed the bottle and spilt vodka everywhere. She just looked at him and started crying like a baby. Danny picked her up off the floor and put her on the armchair.

"Go now," Danny yelled at them all. He went back to the man and saw urine dribbling down his leg. "Look at the fucking mess you're making." All three were laughing at him. The three were all pissed and stoned, easily removable. Somehow Danny managed to throw the two gate crashers out and their rucksacks with them.

"Don't come back." Danny heard them walk down the steps and the door slam.

"Where'd they go?" Chloe slurred, spread out on the bed blown out her head. Danny covered her with a sheet and slumped himself in the arm chair. Fell asleep.

~ ~ ~

The coppice was at twilight melting away to darkness. The clouds hung like a black lead weight about to topple too close for comfort.

Sweating like a pig in his waterproofs sodden inside and out rubbed at his red sore skin. Perched silent and still behind a tree he felt his pulse beat deep and slow behind his ear in the muscle of his neck.

Long slanting ribbons of opaque light filtered through the canopy on the edge of the heath lending an air of melancholia. Birds beat their wings far off in the invisible thicket.

The air smelt damp and rich a heady mix. An owl hooted and he felt the eyes of the wood watching him. But there were other eyes too.

The trees soared higher than church steeples wrestling for the dying of the light. Ancient stumps and moss covered fallen trunks lay with the slope of the heath.

As flashes of light from the distant trunk road filtered through the arches of green lit up his solitude. He was being followed.

The boy's head spun every following footfall thudded and thrummed through the air like a distress code. Sending out a save our souls frequency to run.

On autopilot scrambling down the steep incline an instinctive reaction launched to survival mode. A primeval response in the primeval forest.

Through the faint fog filled well-trodden tracks sliding on wet grass and acorns, bats shrilled and sprayed across his path. Far away children's cries carried on the breeze colliding with his rhythmically wheezing breath.

Clambering through the bushes in the direction of home blinded by endless shrubs and trees. All around him a tangled maze. Can't double back, go left or right. The man was close behind, his dark shadow in the distance.

Deeper into the thicket zig zagging under the canopy of foreboding trees. He slipped down a ditch and under the hedgerow buried his head beneath the brambles.

He could see him searching but he was well hidden. Terrified he heard voices shouting through the evergreen. Could hear his footsteps crunching closer. Reaching the edge of the ditch he stood five feet above him. He never heard him trembling.

Motionless for eternity, hours passed.

Hands and feet grabbing on roots and vines with scratched limbs and scratched face he hauled himself out of the ditch and slumped his body over.

Outside the thicket and on to the heath. Rainfall turned craters and divets into natural puddles and ponds. Where tadpoles gathered and yellow leaves floated upon the surface of their dark deep and still waters.

The flooded meadow submerged by an endless broken tideless sea. He splashed through. Beyond the submergence a carpet of green sludge and decomposition. Over the wall to salvation.

PART SIX

They walked through the park, over the road and then under the subway. They followed the stream of headlights up the road until they reached the industrial estate. They found a narrow alleyway between Bensons for Beds and Toys "R" Us. Then they climbed through a gap in the broken fence, clambered over a large log, and walked down a narrow path which ran waist high through nettles and brambles, treading over plastic bags, beer cans and bottles for about one hundred yards twisting through the woods.

In the depths of the verdant woods vines curled and spread widely, branches dropped heavy with nature's bounty from moss covered boughs. The earth was soft and a hallowed silence spread. Only the shifting sound of their boots and the audible sensation of drizzle which dripped from the green lustrous leaves could be heard. Like jungle explorers they walked the mossy sun lit corridors that threaded the woods.

The setting sun was far away to the west just dipping beneath the tree line. The storm had passed and it was quite mild. As they trudged to the campsite they moved deeper into the woods. Danny spotted a deer; it was the most beautiful animal he had ever set eyes on. They carried on under the canopy of branches and deeper into the labyrinth of green and twisted trees.

Danny tripped on a snag and swung forwards with some momentum and velocity and he tumbled head long down a grassy bank. But something broke his fall because he had a soft landing. Danny picked himself up and brushed himself down, then found himself hearing a gentle squeaking sound as he bounced up and down on the balls of his feet. He looked up to see the other two's heads sticking up above the steep incline.

"Why would someone come all the way out here to dump a mattress?" Danny shouted, bouncing up and down on the springs.

"Satanic worshippers, maybe I don't know!" shouted back Angus.

"What!"

Angus climbed down the bank towards him to take a closer look. The earth was waterlogged, Angus lost his footing, he slipped and landed in thick mud. Kirsty stood at the top of the bank laughing.

Danny started kicking it like an old tyre and pressing down on the springs.

"This is a good mattress," said Danny as he walked around it

"Why don't we take it to the camp?" Danny suggested, then his foot slipped and he fell on it. He just lay on it staring up into the canopy of golden light.

"Comfortable?" Kirsty yelled.

"Really comfortable."

"Liar! We cannae leave it here let's take it back I don't like rubbish in ma back yard, some doggers might use it."

Danny grabbed the corner of the mattress and turned it up on its side. It left a near perfect imprint on the grass and nettles. A few bugs and insects scurried out from underneath. It was wet but apart from that it was in excellent condition, no holes, no springs sticking out. It had a tiny label on it saying Bensons for Beds. They had found themselves a practically brand new double mattress.

"I think it belongs to Benson's Beds," shouted Danny. It may have seemed like they were in the middle of the jungle, but in reality they were just in a large wooded area between the railway line and a large industrial estate on the outskirts of Reading. Danny listened as the sound of the eight thirty two to Newbury sped by.

"That's not Benson's that's mine," she said.

"Damaged stock."

"Benson's dinnae just throw their knackered stock over the wall," said Angus.

"How do you really know?"

"It's big, it won't be easy lugging it up the bank." They tried to move it, Danny took one end Angus the other and they dragged it a few feet up the bank with effort tugging and heaving trying to get a grip but it was damp so their hands kept slipping. Climbing through the brambles and up the ditch, hands and feet grabbing on roots and vines with scratched hands and scratched faces eventually they managed to drag it up and onto the path, but just before they reached the top they toppled over themselves in the process and were panting heavily.

"Leave it," said Angus. He started to walk away.

"No." said Kirsty.

"We can't carry it by ourselves," Danny said.

"You carry it," said Angus.

"Awe an biel ye heid. Do I look like fucking Wonder Woman, are you a man or a mouse go and I'll never speak to you again."

"Promise?"

"Fuck off the wee maggot that ye are."

"Ok." Angus reluctantly walked back.

"If you two lift up the ends I can crawl underneath it, hold it up then we can try to raise it up and balance it on our heads, it may be easier," said Danny.

The others managed to lift the ends a couple of feet off the ground. Danny got on his hands and knees and crawled underneath, taking most of the weight on his back. Then he raised it up using his legs while the others steadied it.

"Are ye alright big man?" said Angus.

"Have yous got it?" he said. It slipped from their grip, Danny slipped underneath on the wet grass. He did the splits then felt his legs click.

"Aaah!" It suddenly went very dark, he landed awkwardly under the mattress and was flattened at an uncomfortable angle. It was crushing him and he could hardly breathe.

"Get it off, please get it off," he yelled. But all he could hear was laughing and giggling in that dark space.

"Shouldn't we help him?" said Kirsty.

"I'd rather leave him. Let's go to Wetherspoons."

"Come on I'm trapped I can't breathe," he shouted.

Suddenly he heard muffled screaming, then the screech of brakes and then a ringing bell.

"Get out the road, get out the road." Someone on a bicycle hurtling towards them. Danny felt an almighty weight land on him. "Fuck. Aaah." Then the sound of crashing metal.

"Ah my fucking back," Danny yelled.

"Shit my fucking bike," said the rider. Danny felt someone walking all over him.

"What the fuck are you doing you could have killed me," said the rider.

"Craigie Boy," said Angus.

"Angus, Kirsty."

"Get me out get me out," Danny screamed, he was in a very uncomfortable position and his backside was getting very wet. "Come on guys please. What the fucks going on you using me as a bouncy castle, get me out it's not funny anymore." Danny was losing air and his back and legs were killing him.

"Who are ye?" said Kirsty.

"It's Craigie Boy, you know Craigie Boy he used to work in the kitchen at the centre. Auch ye know."

"No."

"He used to dance like a wee chicken 'bwah! bwah!'" Angus was clucking and crowing like a chicken trying to prick Kirsty's memory. "Bwah, bwah… you remember you danced like a chicken behind the counter. Why don't you come to the kitchen anymore?"

"I work at the hospital now. Kitchen porter."

"Good pay?" Angus asked.

"Eleven quid an hour, but it's enough to live on, maybe I could get you a job."

It went quiet for a minute then Danny heard the sound of metal banging, a bicycle being wheeled over then someone spinning a wheel. Then he felt someone prodding the mattress.

"It's alright no damage," said Kirsty.

"That's not the same for my bike it's fucking ruined."

"Auch I'll get you another bike, nae borra pal."

"Are you stoned?" asked Kirsty.

"No," Craigie replied.

"I remember you now, proper pot head, got asked to leave for smoking weed in the pisser," said Kirsty.

"Bollocks that weren't me."

"Aye ye bums oot the windae, like a fart in a trance man."

"I didn't expect to run into to idiots carrying their bed through the woods."

"Well it gave you a soft landing, you want some weed?"

"I don't smoke weed… Well sometimes. Just a little, stress, stress of work. I sometimes envy you lot. You've got no responsibility you're free living rough under the stars with just a tent no one telling you what to do."

"Do you? Aye."

"I'd love to be free sometimes."

"Why not leave, you could do anything, go anywheres Angus.

"Like what"

"Look at wee Archie he went all the way to Egypt to paint the pyramids."

"What colour?" said Kirsty.

"Auch."

"I can't paint. But I'm good at DIY."

"No you cannae go all the way to Egypt just to put shelves up"

"For fucks sake, will somebody get this fucking mattress off me now!!" said Craigie. Finally they stopped jabbering and lifted the mattress off Danny. Danny saw all three of them staring down at him. He tried to pick himself up but his back spasmed, eventually he got to his feet. His whole body felt as stiff as a board. Kirsty pulled an exasperated expression and raised her eyes.

"Let's go," she said.

"Awrite ye bawbag."

They watched Craigie wheel his broken bike away. Angus helped them reluctantly, shaking his head and cursing under his breath like he had Tourette's. It was slowly getting dark and a full moon was rising through the clouds as they staggered under the canopy. Trampling undergrowth and making dead branches snap, nits danced in the air and in their hair, making them itch. Danny saw something lurking in the gloom. A creature of the night perhaps a rabbit beside the edge of the brook they went, sweating their path to the west.

They took on a more urgent pace beside the flow of water and now the moon had finally revealed itself and they could see far more clearly. The small brook had grown into a river, they had to stop to catch their breaths.

Eventually they came to a small clearing above a steep incline, a small enclave with a collection of tents thick with the glow of fireflies. In the middle of the clearing stood a lightning petrified tree, primeval, prostrate and charred, its gnarled branches stretched out malignantly. Under the caws of crows, twilight threw its cloak over the ramshackle campsite and wreathed the tops of the trees in a dissipating golden halo.

Miles from anywhere, covered with holes in the earth and soot from burned out fires. Torn down sticks and branches scattered the floor with other rubbish debris. Old mugs and kettles were dumped on the earth. Then they dumped the mattress on the earth next to their shopping, as they called it, various stolen goods from the shopping centre, under a plastic sheet.

A memorial had been constructed from a couple of branches tied together with some rope in the shape of a cross. They were mourning the recent death of their dog, which was buried in the earth. The anguish of its death cut deep within them, flowering weeds adorned the graveside and were spread over the base of the tree.

Night was drawing in and the wind whistled through the branches. Kirsty gathered more twigs sticks and brambles and started a fire.

Angus sat down on the log by the fire warming himself. He raised a bottle of Bushmills and toasted the dog.

"Ye gonna join us in a wee swally Danny?" He offered the bottle to him. Danny shook his head. "I don't drink."

"Auch since when?"

"One hundred and eighty four days ago but who's counting."

They were warm and friendly. They weren't normal but he cherished their welcoming spirit.

As the heat rose steadily through the early hours it was not possible to unzip the tent door for fear of being eaten alive by bugs. Danny had two choices. He could slowly boil like an egg and drown in the sea of his perspiration, or unzip the flap which offered precious little air and the threat of insect invasion.

The faint delicate strains of insects gently humming fell upon his ears, measure after increasing measure it flowed unabated around his tent. Gentle in its cadences the tent tremblingly in its vibration. A moth rose and fluttered against the roof of his tent glistening purple its wings gently stirred the humid air.

Danny saw a greyish hue penetrate through a hole above the zipper in the flap. He grabbed the torch light and saw the ceiling of the tent was covered with bugs, luminous in the torch light. Most of the ceiling was invisible under the swarm of writhing and crawling interlopers. One fell to his body followed by a few others falling with a fleshy thud.

Gradually the hideous wall of creeping flesh crept downwards enticed by the torch light and took to wing around him. They started to dart and stab aiming without provocation at his face and eyes, crawling up his nose, ears and the corner of his mouth. Infesting the bed clothes with their droning poisoned assault on his senses, the space brimming with the expectation of attack bent on his annihilation.

In seconds his body was covered in a thick black moving rug, many underneath his garments the bite of their sharp mandibles became intolerable. He had to flee.

The mist of bugs that surrounded the coppice was buzzing all around him, curtaining the trees and weaving its dark silky thread through the branches. The trees were fighting a losing battle against the invading parasites craving sustenance and sucking the life blood out of the coppice.

Attracted by the fetid stench of rotten food they flew in a thick black cloud from the boughs of the trees and descended to the dank enclave floor, zealously gobbling the decay; the only thing that defied the onslaught was the petrified tree. Danny headed deep into the woods to find Salvation.

~ ~ ~

Their high pitched squeals drove splinters into his tortured brain. All around him crawled the hideous creatures so closely amassed their shapes indeterminate. Hiding in the hay his nostrils full of their musty stench.

The barn was full of swine staring up at him mouths gaping and hungry. Their dark shadows moved in strange undulations. He felt like a small boat afloat on a dark turbulent sea. They crowded beneath him dead eyes staring into his, out of reach out of sight

The torch that wavered in the man's hand hardly pierced the darkness, the beam swept over the mud and straw, over the backs of the sweaty pigs and through the air thick with flies

The pigs stirred uncomfortably in their pens, the light on the wall was switched. Squealing rang fire all over the barn as the pigs reared up in their confinement. Pigs possess none of the silent curiosity of cattle.

The long narrow barn lit by long wavering lights suspended by wires from the ceiling moved in the draft from the open door. The contours of the pens full of writhing swine pushing snouts through the bars of their cages. The deafening squeals underlain by a cacophony of grunting he stayed hidden in the hay.

The men searched the pig house, their conversation inaudible above the racket. The lights were flicked, in darkness again. He felt someone stroking his hair.

~ ~ ~

Morning and the sun's rays cascaded through the lush green trees encasing the camp strewing its golden glow on the forest floor. Angus sat on a fallen log with knot hole eye sockets to match his own, his curly black mop in the dappled sunlight blowing in the breeze. He looked as white as a sheet, nervous and twitching his phone shaking in his hand.

"Morning big man," said Angus.

"You look how I feel."

"It's all over fucking You Tube."

"What is?"

"Me, waving mae big babookie in the park."

"No way." He passed his phone to Danny and he watched the wonky video.

"She filmed me on her phone, uploaded it, it went viral millions of people have seen it… that gives me the boak I'm proper scunnerd wae her."

"You're famous."

"Shut your geggy…the skanky wee bitch spiked mae tobacco, fucked mae heid up."

"Where is she?"

"Done a bunk. Mae heid is splitten, I was pure maed wae it last night… delusional."

"Where did she go?"

"I don't care I dannae wanna see her again…fugly nugget, she can fuck off forever."

"Really?"

"Aye. Do ye think am buttoned up the back?"

"She's beautiful."

"Aye well, I wisnae gonna chuck her out of bed if you know what mean… Mad Jakey stole me stash by the way."

~ ~ ~

Danny took the letter out of his pocket. Everything had been reduced to this single purpose. To confront Peter one last time. But he wasn't sure what he hoped to achieve by such an encounter.

Peter was reaching out for forgiveness. He knew he had to confront him and that nothing would be settled until he did. He needed to exorcise the ghost or he would be haunted forever.

He wasn't sure how he would react if he had the courage to see him. The murderous fantasies that had consumed him were just that. But the power he still held over him had to be smashed. The fear of facing him had turned him into a prisoner locking him into a world of anger, loneliness and fear. He had been given the key; he just had to put it in the lock and turn the key.

~ ~ ~

Peter looked fully into Danny's eyes, seared into them, and responded to Danny's visible state of fear with unadulterated pleasure. A fervour glowered within Peter and burned like a blow torch into Danny's mind.

A faint tremble passed through Danny's limbs as Peter gazed through his cold dark eyes into his transparent soul. Peter had no doubt in his mind that he still wielded power and fear over Danny like an axe, even after all these years.

A thin smile of self-satisfaction passed over Peter's thin cracked lips and he derived pleasure from Danny's discomfort. Not unlike when he was a child.

"Sorry about your sister, she was such a sweet little thing as I recall," Peter said. With such over familiarity Danny responded like the child he had reverted to in his presence.

"Thanks." A terrible image flashed through his mind. He repressed his reaction; it was fleeting and soon gone. What was he thinking? Why had he agreed to come, he wasn't deserving of his forgiveness. Why was he talking to this man who wrought such pain and suffering into his life, who fuelled his nightmares? For all the intimate familiarity Danny contained a demeanour so rigid in its resolve.

With eyes that conveyed secrets from the depths of one soul to the depths of another as if they were so dark they could hardly be whispered. Danny shuddered at the returning images that rose monster like from the cavern of his soul. Danny stared at him hard and his hatred grew like the storm that battered the window. He knew him beyond all others' knowledge.

Peter had been incarcerated between four walls most of his miserable life. Danny had been infected by his poison most of his life, until his entire nature had been the deadliest toxin in existence. Unlike the rot in an apple, he couldn't cut it out or remove it. It just grew inside him like a cancer slowly devouring him from within. The poison of Peter's breath blasted the clogged air.

Danny tried to conceal his emotions but the underlying tone in which he spoke about his sister was torture to his spirit.

As Peter grinned at him like a demon possessed Danny strove hard to quell them. Peter watched with suspicion the prison guard who sat in the corner of the room.

A moment ago the power Peter had over him was merciless; he felt withered at his glance, but he managed to shake it off. His inner fears quelled into sullen indifference. Then Peter's rage broke forth like a lightning flash from a thunder cloud.

"You have severed me from all the warmth of life, left me to rot in this stinking hole. You did this to me. Look, they cut half my ears off."

Peter thrusted his face forward, pulled his hair away from his ears to reveal his mutilated lobes. The prison guard stood up, walked forwards. Peter sat down and Danny raised his hand to the guard in a demonstration of peace. He returned to the corner of the room.

You're poison. You filled me with poison, you made me as hateful and ugly and as loathsome as yourself Danny thought but he wouldn't admit it.

"Why did you want to see me? I thought you were looking for forgiveness. Wanted to say sorry."

"Oh I'm so so sorry," he derided. "You poor child. I loved you. I thought you loved me too."

"It's a beautiful day outside. I don't hate you, in fact I never think about you. You mean nothing to me. Water under the bridge."

"So why did you come?" Danny shrugged. He realised it was a waste of time; Peter wasn't looking for forgiveness it was just a sick game.

"I pity you, you're just a sad pathetic broken old man with nothing to live for.

~ ~ ~

Outside the prison gates the wind had dropped, the air smelt fresh and pure. He breathed it in like sweet nectar, the taste of freedom. The fear was gone, replaced only by a sense of peace and tranquillity. He didn't know what the future held. Who does?

God grant me the serenity to accept the things I cannot change. The courage to change the things I can and the wisdom to know the difference.

Reinhold Niebuhr

~ ~ ~

Printed in Dunstable, United Kingdom